There's No Such Thing as an Inadequate Man

Irving Schiffer

For those locked away inside themselves:
The key is in reach; use it.

But now and then he preferred to give vent to astonishment at riches, because there was something unreal and ridiculous about too much wealth.

— Irving Schiffer, *A Great Place to Visit*

CHAPTER 1

Bart Seeley stalked into Eunice Pratt's boarding house and walked through the parlor, which was a large room meant to assault a man's senses, a place of needlework, samplers, chintz, old-lady creation in cloth all over the walls and things that looked like small looms...a small house run by square women, Nelly and her widowed mother. He found Nelly in the dining room, laying out the silver for breakfast. She was an extremely ugly girl with buck teeth like a horse, and he had always been convinced she was on the simple side. He therefore wasted no time on courtesy before he asked her to direct him to Morrison's room. Morrison was the big man.

Bart had violent feelings about big men. He was short himself, wide and powerful; simian, in fact, even in the hanging length of his arms, and he hated big men even more fiercely than he hated most other men.

He was short and he was balding too. Although only twenty-five, he was bald way back on his head. As only balding men can, he held that this was indeed a sign of virility, because women never became bald, did they?

He was by no means an intelligent man, yet he held a remarkably powerful position in the town of Greenville. No one knew why he had been so blessed, least of all Bart himself. When he was a youngster, his greatest sport was bullying Lance Harper whenever possible. Lance was Janet Harper's only son. And she owned the town. So how could you figure that one out?

He could remember his own parents—rest in peace— imploring him to leave Lance alone. Had the wealthy boy's mother taken it into her hands to do so, after all, she could easily have ruined them all. But young Bart was driven by his own passions, not his mother's entreaties, and Bart had not stopped taunting Lance, and Janet Harper had not retaliated. Bart had prospered. He had, indeed, been made employment director for all her factories and was allowed to operate a debt collection agency that bordered on outright gangsterism.

Managing this lucrative business and the Harper factories' employment office in the center of town, Bart enjoyed an unbridled exercise of power. It was said that if he hated a man, that man had no chance of obtaining a job in any business enterprise in the town of Greenville. Such had been his intention for Morrison, who had applied for a factory job the day before. It was infuriating to find that he was not to have his way with this man.

As he pounded his fist on the upstairs door to which Nelly had directed him, he cursed richly under his breath. *Shit*, he didn't have to run errands for Janet Harper. He'd done enough for her, and they were in a mess of trouble now. Shared trouble, whether she liked it or not. And anyway, what in hell did she want with this Morrison lug? She didn't know the man. Of that he was quite certain, in as much as she had referred to him over the phone as the big man who had come out of the employment office just before closing yesterday. At best, she'd only seen Morrison at a distance. What the hell! Bart thought.

One thing he hated was being sent on errands. Especially today. Especially after what had happened. He pounded on the door with all his rage and might.

In a moment, the door opened. The man stood there stripped to the waist and looked down at him. Bart glared belligerently. He knew that Morrison was his own age, but Bart looked much older.

"You Morrison?"

"Sure."

The man contemplated him with curiosity.

"I was in your office last night, remember?" Morrison said flatly.

"Your office." That was respectful. One thing about this giant, he had been awful respectful yesterday. He was a little kid under all that muscle.

"You think I remember every jerk who comes into my office?" Bart growled. "Well, you gonna let me in? I gotta talk to you."

Morrison opened the door wider and let him in.

"Close it."

Morrison closed the door and stood waiting. Bart walked to the center of the room and studied the man.

It was incredible. The man was built like some kind of statue. The face was like rock. In all his secret fantasies about the physical perfection he aspired to, Bart Seely had never conceived of such a specimen. And he had never been so envious and so frustrated as he was at this moment. He had never, he was certain, hated so vehemently.

And never had he felt this futility in the knowledge that there was nothing he could do about the emotions strangling him. He had never met a big man he hadn't wanted to fight, and he rarely fought without winning. But good sense told him that he could not overcome this man in physical combat. He was afraid even to speak for a moment lest his frustration bring a whine to his voice. The thought of sounding like Lance Harper, whom he had caused to whine often at an early age, made him shudder.

"You know Janet Harper?" he blurted finally.

Morrison was slow, it seemed. "She the one who owns this town?"

"That's right. You know her?"

"Afraid not," said Morrison, shrugging a pair of astonishingly wide shoulders.

"You sure?"

The big man raised a craggy brow and declined to answer. With the instinct of the fearful, Bart Seely hurried to fill the silence.

"She wants to see you..."

"Hmm, is that right."

"You sure you don't know why, Morrison?"

"How does she know me?"

"That's what I was wondering." Bart smirked. He stepped back and inspected the big man speculatively, but in his voice, he strove for the modulation of masculine camaraderie. "Maybe she wants to get laid, eh? You sure you never laid her?"

Morrison had dark brown eyes. They weren't as easy to read as some other eyes, but Bart was surprised that he could read no anger there at all. Another man's eyes would have said something, and some men might even have knocked him down.

"Maybe you laid Vicki once," Bart suggested, emboldened. "A lot of people have laid Vicki. She's Mrs. Harper's daughter. In New Orleans right now. Maybe you come from New Orleans..."

"When and where does she want to see me?"

"She'll see you at her house. Go to the servants' entrance. Right away. Right away, I said."

Morrison digested this. A lot depended on what the big man did now, Bart decided. But he was astonished that the man offered a slow, easy smile.

"If it's for a job in one of her factories," he said agreeably, "tell her I'll be there in ten minutes."

Bart stood there; his lips tightened. "I don't know what it's for. I told you that. But I got orders to get you there. I'll get you there even if I have to carry you."

Morrison didn't respond to that one either. He got tiny white lines around his mouth, like scratches on a rock, but he didn't move in or show annoyance or anything. Bart waited a full minute. Another man would have thrown him out of the door in that time. Assuming that another man could. Morrison evidently could not. Bart stepped forward.

"I don't like big jerks," he stated.

He was up close, and it seemed to him now that those dark eyes had finally registered what he liked most to see in a pair of eyes. But this was different. He had a feeling that it was something more than cowardly fear; that it was something like resignation. But he didn't care much: it was a fighting look. So he swung.

The first one was a right that caught Morrison in the stomach. He waited for the big man to go down. Morrison grunted. Bart hit him with the right again, in the neck this time. Morrison gasped and bent double, covering his face with bulging arms, and started to back away. Bart followed and caught him high on the head. The big man kept backing away.

But he didn't go down. He soon stopped moving away because a wall was behind him, and he didn't lift a hand to fight. But his legs never buckled.

Bart, his eyes shining, stood so close that he breathed down on the crouching figure. Gleefully, he placed his blows, putting his entire body behind each of them. He went for the ears and the nape and the kidneys because he couldn't get to the face or the breadbasket. His dancing feet were springy as he circled between blows. With each of them, he grunted and sometimes laughed.

The man he was beating uttered nothing, not a sound. The man crouched and waited under the shelter of his own gigantic arms, his sculptural body glistening with sweat. For Bart Seely, the pleasure of striking the man was so extreme as to approach something sexual—hearing the thud of his fist as it bounced off the man's hard skin, feeling the muscular twistings of his own trunk muscles as his arm went forward, the flowing coordination of his back and shoulder muscles....

A low rumble began in Bart's throat. Before he knew it, he was laughing. Then, suddenly, he was exhausted and weak and full of a terrible fear. He realized in horror that he had not hurt the big man. He stopped hitting. He began to tremble, and now an awful sound was coming from his own mouth, a kind of babbling and sobbing.

"What the hell kind of man are you?" he screamed at the heaving back. "I can't—I—"

"You finished?" said Morrison, not even turning around or standing up from his bent position.

For a moment, Bart Seely stood swaying, wide-eyed, his throat working as though he had something to say but had lost his voice.

He could see the big man's muscles relaxing like clay melting on a statue. He stared another moment and then ran from the room.

★★★

Janet gazed appreciatively at the big man. He was quite up to expectations. She had not seen him close enough the evening before to determine whether he was handsome, although that was hardly of any importance. In the dream last night, he had been a faceless symbol of masculinity, a silhouette of power and austere ruggedness, certainly not beauty. Now, studying his face with all the candor and brazenness of a child (or someone who was insolently rich), she was almost ecstatic at what she beheld. He was not, of course, handsome, not in any of the classic ways; on such a man, that kind of face would have been repulsive. But this face? How would she describe this man's face?

It was like a mask. One did not imagine that there were fleshy muscles or blood-filled nerves and capillaries beneath the rock-like texture of the skin. One did not suppose that he could produce or control a variety of expressions upon that granite countenance; the jutting hardness of brows, nose and chin could not be his—his the way most people own and have intimacy with their own features. Nor could any man conceivably have the hardness and serenity of character to match such a face. It seemed to her a desecration that those features were mobile at all, could be at all expressive. Yet they were, even if in a fashion too subtle to understand, or else how was it that she was able to discern the one thing she had not expected to find, the one thing she would still not believe, a kind of pained sensitivity. Yet that, too, was possible: behind such a mask a man could hide anything—the deepest feelings, the deepest intelligence, or incredible genius. She knew that she might be reading too much into this man seated so obediently across from her because he was, after all, the man in The Dream last night.

"Morrison," she said, and she decided to repeat the name, to let him know that she was testing it and that it was necessary for her to test things and to feel them before deciding whether she liked them. "Morrison. Yes, I suppose you'll do very well for the job."

"What job, ma'am?" he asked in a perfectly even voice.

"Can you drive?" When he said yes to this, she shot at him with disarming casualness. "And dancing—can you do ordinary social dancing?"

He nodded to that, almost sadly. He seemed to know that it would make no difference if he said he couldn't drive or dance. She felt the urge to put out her hand to him and tell him that he needn't be sad, but of course she couldn't do that. She jangled the collection of bracelets on her left hand noisily and said, "That's fine. We'll get you some good clothes this afternoon. I'll have William see a few people about it today, even though it's Sunday. Do you have a suit or two meanwhile?"

"I'm wearing it," said Morrison, tapping his hand at his serviceable gray tweed. "I wasn't planning on dressing up much in the factory."

"Factory?"

"That's what I thought you wanted me for, Mrs. Harper, a job in one of your factories. Lathe, maintenance, foreman, anything—"

"Oh." She certainly didn't intend to argue the point. "Well, no factory, I'm afraid. I've decided you'll be more useful here."

"I'd prefer a factory job," said Morrison.

She raised her thin face and flicked at her blonde hair as though to rid herself of some little insect. Her mouth moved quickly in sharp enunciation. She was only forty-three, but sometimes she could be as brittle and indignant as an old woman. "Morrison, get this straight. I like independence, I like it well enough, no real objection to it.

There'll be room for it later on, I promise you. But you must understand that I am the one who says—I'm the one to decide who has what job in Greenville. Is that clear?"

He looked at her silently for several seconds. She watched in fascination as his bloodless lips opened to reveal strong and very white teeth.

"How do you know me?" he asked. "How'd you happen to call me here?"

"That's easy enough to answer. I saw you in town yesterday," she answered candidly. "You were quite an impressive figure. You should see yourself some day at a distance of a hundred yards or so."

"Was that meant to be flirtatious, Mrs. Harper?"

"Perhaps," she said, smiling.

"Suppose I don't want the job," he said.

By this time, she knew she had been unnecessarily coarse. She also knew that what he'd just said was an experiment; he wasn't really testing the extent of her power and influence—he believed that—but rather the dimensions of her will. For an instant, she was tempted to bring her will and all its wrath down upon him, but she quickly decided that the bother of being angry wasn't at all necessary.

"Don't want the job?" she asked pleasantly. "Why shouldn't you? Most men would give their eye teeth for such easy work."

"What work?"

Her laugh was genuine, spiraling high before it fell. "I did forget to mention that, didn't I? My oh my. Let's call you a companion."

"You got an invalid in the house?"

She pondered his question and screwed up her face in a manner that hid her real annoyance. She pressed a bell under her desk and said shortly, "Something like that, Morrison. Now, this afternoon, you'll attend a tea party in the music room. Yes, I said tea party. You'll attend so that we can establish to everybody that you're not just a hired man. Tomorrow, however, you'll be the chauffeur for awhile and you'll take the car to the airport in Jefferson, where you'll pick up my daughter. William will give you directions if you need them."

A pretty brunette in a maid's uniform, a somehow faded girl (though she couldn't have been over thirty), came quietly along the hall just then.

"Diane, this is Morrison," Janet Harper said, hardly glancing at the maid. "He'll use the extra guest room in the right wing. Have Sommers get his belongings from Eunice Pratt's house and bring them to his room."

The maid glanced indifferently at Morrison. Her indifference took in a lot. "Is that all, ma'am?"

"No. Show him his room first." Janet turned to look up at the young man. "Unless you'd rather come to church with me?"

"No thanks," he said.

"Then you can lunch in your room if you wish. Just ring for Diane. The tea is at one o'clock, so you'll want to settle yourself before then. Have Sommers press your suit."

"All right," he said.

"Everything clear, Morrison?"

"I suppose so," he said.

He was sprawled on a large green bedspread a half-hour later, smoking and dropping his cigarette ashes on a deep green broadloom, when the butler and the chauffeur dragged in his gear. The butler, Sommers, looked like a prig; Morrison sent him out after changing himself into a pair of jeans and giving the butler the suit to press. The chauffeur was little and gray, though not really old, and appeared to be a right guy. Morrison detained him.

"Sit down, sit down," Morrison invited.

The elderly chauffeur settled uncertainly into a tufted chair and folded one bony knee over the other.

"Cigarette?" Morrison asked, not moving to offer one. The chauffeur shook his head. "What's your name, then?"

"William Peltz," said the old gentleman.

"All right, Mr. Peltz, I'm Morrison. I'm the new companion."

The man looked quite blank.

Morrison pursued it. "Mrs. Harper hired me as the new companion. What happened to her other companions?"

"Companions, sir?"

"Mrs. Harper's boyfriends."

William blushed. "But she never had any boyfriends. I'm quite sure of that, quite sure. Since her husband's death—and that means since the children were little—Mrs. Harper has, at least from what I've heard—there have been no...."

Morrison tossed his cigarette out the open window. "Well, then, I don't get it. Peltz, what could she do if I refuse to work for her?"

"But I'm sure—"

He sat straight up in the bed. "Don't be sure of anything. Just tell me what she could do if she wanted to."

The chauffeur smiled. "Could, sir? She could do anything. The police are usually very cooperative with her. So is the governor. So is—"

"That's what I figured. Listen, Peltz, I'm taking over your job tomorrow morning."

The chauffeur went white. Morrison grinned at him.

"Christ, I didn't mean to scare you that way. You always so jumpy? No, not permanently taking it over, just to pick up Mrs. Harper's daughter at the airport."

William smiled weakly. "You did kind of unsettle me. Yes, I heard from Diane that Vicki is coming home."

"This Vicki—is she an invalid?"

"Invalid? No, certainly not that, sir."

"How old?"

"Twenty-one, I believe. I've been here a few years myself, and I've seen very little of her. She's home so seldom."

"What kind of girl is she that makes her certainly not like an invalid?"

William was blushing again.

"Go on, please," said Morrison.

"Well—undisciplined, you might say."

"Wild?"

William couldn't deny it.

"Who else is there? In this house, I mean."

"The son, Lance. He came home a few days ago. He also goes away all the time." The chauffeur brightened suddenly. "Perhaps he could be considered an invalid."

Morrison was all attention. "That's good news. What's wrong with him?"

"He drinks."

"How old?"

"Twenty-five, twenty-six..."

"Well, he's drinking in the cottage, I imagine."

"Hiding from his mother?"

"No sir. She knows."

Morrison jumped from the bed. He hadn't bothered to remove his shoes in the first place, and the bedspread would never forget him. "Just show me the cottage, Peltz. I'll take it from there. You're a good friend."

The chauffeur pointed through the window to a low-slung structure far back on the lawn under some trees.

It was full of windows with screens, Morrison observed, as he approached across the lawn. When he stood at the door, he heard a scuffling inside. It was too dark in there to see a thing.

"Mother?" came a querulous voice. When there was no answer, the voice dropped a pitch, guardedly. "Who's there? Mother?"

"Not your mother," he answered, ducking his head to step inside. "Just a friend."

Familiarizing his eyes to the darkness, Morrison made out a very slim man with a blond cowlick over half his face lounging in an upholstered bamboo beach chair. He was nursing a bottle, the grown-up kind.

"Heyyy-yyy!" the man cried out. "What're you doing here? Get the hell off this property."

The bottle was half empty and Lance wasn't slurring a word. But he was drunk, all right; the head was lolling, the eyelids were heavy. Morrison doubted that he could get off the chair.

"You hold that stuff pretty well," he said admiringly.

"Drop dead. Drop dead, drop dead, drop dead," sang the boy-man.

"You going to finish that whole bottle?"

"Get the hell out of here, I said."

"Just wanted to introduce myself. Morrison's the name, and I've got a funny notion that it's going to be my job to kind of take care of you."

Lance Harper told him what he could do to himself.

"Later," Morrison said amicably, walking toward him. "Is this what you do all day?"

Lance cringed in his chair. The big man shrugged.

"Listen, I'm not going to hurt you. After all, I'm no older than you, so I'd better have respect, right? I'll bet you've got a couple of months up on me."

The limp man didn't answer. Morrison stood over him for a moment and was about to turn to leave when he saw a shadow come into the doorway.

"What do you think you're doing?" Janet Harper demanded.

He turned slowly, facing the slender, nervous silhouette. The sun in the back of her showed somehow that the blonde hair was bleached, but there in the doorway she looked like a younger woman than she was. Her tone of voice, however, was authoritative and not so young.

"I saw you coming out here," she said accusingly. "Keep away from Lance, do you hear me? Lance, don't be upset..."

Morrison glanced at the other man, who seemed to be cringing. "Sorry," he said, facing Janet. "I thought maybe he was my job."

"He's not," she hissed, looking at him with something like hate.

"That's real bad news," he said, walking past her out of the cottage.

She followed. She put a hand on his arm and made him stand still in the morning sun.

"I guess you meant well," she said. "But he—he needs the drinking. It makes him forget he's such a weak young man."

"He needs you to mama him, you mean," he said carelessly.

She blinked her eyes a few moments, then shook her head. "You just don't understand. Anyway, I can't change him. I can let him be happy, at least."

He looked down at her hand and saw her arm was loaded with bracelets. She removed her clawlike fingers from his arm and sighed. "Actually, I came looking for you because the police are here to see you."

"The police? What do they want with me?"

"They wouldn't tell me. They want to speak with you alone. They're in the library."

He followed her to the library, a rich room like something out of the movies—a high ceiling that featured long wooden beams, deep brown against white ceilings, stark and strange. It also featured two uniformed state policemen, one of them a head taller than the other. As if leaving him to his fate, she excused herself and departed without another word.

"Are you Morrison?"

"Yes, I am. What's wrong?"

The short policeman winced as though the question had been presumptuous. He had hair growing out of his ears and a sardonic look, as though constantly annoyed at the bad manners people exhibited. "Why don't you sit down so we can talk easier."

Morrison followed the instructions. Both policemen seemed to take note of his size as he lowered himself.

"How'd you get into town?"

"I rode in," said Morrison. "Got a lift."

"Yeah, that's what we heard. Where'd your friend go?"

"The guy whose car it was? He wasn't my friend. It was just a lift. He picked me up in Tulliver County. I hitchhiked up here. His name was Ned Amsterdam, I think."

"You think right. Did you see him after he dropped you off yesterday?"

"No. Why, is he in trouble?"

"What makes you say that?"

Morrison shrugged. "I guess he is in trouble, then."

"He's dead," said the tall policeman. The other one turned on his partner and winced as if to say he should have withheld the news so they could continue the cat and mouse.

"Sorry to hear that," Morrison offered. "I'll be glad to tell you whatever I know. Was it an accident?" He looked from one to the other. "Or was it something else?"

"We'll do the questioning, Morrison, if you don't mind. He left you off at the boarding house in town, right?"

"That's right."

"Did you see him after that?"

"No. I told you. He drove off."

"All right, kid, I'll answer your questions," said the tall one. "He was killed, murdered. It was sometime yesterday evening, the coroner says. If you didn't leave town once you got here yesterday, then you couldn't have done it. We found him and his car about ten miles out of town. We got your name from Nelly at the boarding house, and from what we hear, you came in and stayed in, except for going over to the employment office."

Morrison let out his breath. "Well, I'm glad I'm covered."

"Got some identification?" asked the short policeman.

They waited, on alert, while he reached for his wallet. He extracted a driver's license and his army discharge papers and handed them over. The short one copied the information in a notebook.

"Vietnam?" he asked.

Morrison nodded.

"We'll check you out," he promised. "You live in the city?" he added, noting the address. "What kind of work do you do?" The tall policeman scratched his forehead thoughtfully over Morrison's apparent hesitation.

"I did all kinds of work. Construction, everything."

"Is that right?" said the short one who had hair in his ears, obviously not believing him. "Did you take anything from the car?"

Morrison's eyes were calm. "I told you—he left me off in town. He said he was coming here to see a friend."

"Did he mention any names?"

"No, that's all he said."

"You came here for a job, is that it? Nelly says you were looking for a job."

"That's right."

"Why this town?"

"No reason. It was just where this guy Amsterdam was going."

"And you didn't take anything from the car?"

"No, I didn't. I told you; he was a very nice guy who gave me a lift."

"No fight? How come you're beginning to get a little swelling on the side of your jaw?"

Morrison looked away. "That was somebody else," he said, his voice barely audible.

"You had a fight with somebody else? Who?"

"His name is Seely."

"Bart Seely? From the collection agency?"

"He runs the employment office in town."

"Oh yeah, he runs everything... He beat you up like that?"

The cops looked at each other. One shrugged at the other.

"How come? What'd you fight about?"

Morrison shook his head. "I don't really know," he said.

Each of you is one of many group members who want to share a mystical moment with others... become aware of your senses...feel the texture of leaves and silk and someone's hands. Close your eyes and touch. You are welcome to our Happiness Club. You cannot grow in a vacuum, without physical contact. There is meeting and meeting, touching and touching. If you are defensive, then you touch no one; out of fear, you execute an end run, which takes you away from others and from yourself. Close your eyes. Now touch hands with the one next to you... Into the center of the circle...bump anyone who tries to share the center with you. Now...touch her face and her arms. Do you like the feel of her skin? Stroke her hair. If you care to become more intimate in your touch, any of you, go ahead and do so...

CHAPTER 2

Carlotta Ford was perhaps the most beautiful human being ever to live in the town of Greenville as transient or resident, devil or angel, male or female. Since the age of fifteen, she had been invited to every party and every girlish secret of any importance in a town that had many parties and secrets. She was now twenty-one, and her beauty had reached an apogee of perfection that left her spinning near the very edge of isolation where all she experienced seemed unsatisfactory and anticlimactic—because beauty alone will take the human spirit only so far. Her hair was black and of remarkable luster; her skin was as near to a transparent covering of marble as skin could be; her legs were long and thin; her eyes were gray of a shade that seemed lightly sketched in with charcoal on a pure white vellum. She was utterly feminine and restrained at once. She was a virgin.

She was also rich; that is, her father, Ambrose Ford, was rich, because he was the general manager of Janet Harper's soda and bottling works. Growing up, Carlotta had been Vicki Harper's closest friend. To cement this friendship for reasons of her own, Vicki's mother had gone so far as to have Carlotta sent to the same private school in Jefferson where Vicki studied so that, Janet explained, her daughter might have a constant friend and protector in Carlotta.

That, more or less, was why Carlotta's father was a rich man today. And due in part to such a flattering history, Carlotta had never been known to lose her poise in any situation or with any man she had met since adolescence. She was the kind of girl who could let a man think he was boring her when, as it happened, he was. She appeared to have no fear and no reason to fear anything.

What she felt now was probably the only brand of uneasiness she knew—a slight apprehension, annoyance—because there was something in this room of which everyone seemed to be aware but of which no one had informed Carlotta Ford.

Sipping her tea, she told herself that there was nothing that was strange. Here she was, seated with dignity in a straight-back chair at one of Janet's ridiculous Sunday teas. A usual Sunday afternoon place to be. Every Sunday, in fact. It was fantastic that such a weekly institution could still exist in the 1970s, that Janet could actually still call them tea parties, probably not even aware that marijuana was sometimes the real tea that was consumed at her low-key parties. Yet here she was.

The sun, as usual, streamed into the spacious music room, glistening on the ebony piano, on the fine, translucent teacups and the bland faces of most of the socially acceptable and unmarried persons of Greenville and some from Jefferson and even beyond that. All the girls she had been allowed to grow up with were there, except Vicki, of course, who had been in New Orleans almost a year. All the usual young men were present. Lance was home, back from his neurotic trips on freight trains. Nothing was really different, nothing to account for the tenseness. Nothing except the big man.

Was that the answer? Was there some choice bit of gossip about this man that had not reached her ears?

He was the only stranger in the room, and she had never seen a man so out of place in any locale as this giant moving about the music room. Despite herself she had been watching him, admiring him. For there was something about him.

The garrulous Tim Hoyt, she observed shudderingly, seemed even more infantile and boastful and backslapping than ever in the presence of the new man, though it did not occur to him to slap the big man on the back or anywhere else. Harry Giles, who had been living off his father's stock in the bottling works, who wore horn-rimmed glasses and was supposedly writing a play, had never rung out his voice so pompously, had never been so obnoxious. The whining tones of Lance Harper and his surreptitious attempts to pour whiskey from a hidden flask into everyone else's teacup (drunkards and weaklings want so much to share their weaknesses)—all of these young men had somehow today characterized themselves more clearly than all the muddled impressions of the years she had known them.

With astonishment, Carlotta realized that what had taken her a lifetime in Greenville to learn about its inhabitants had probably taken the unknown visitor thirty minutes or so, or however long the party had been going on. Yet the big man had done nothing to cause tension and acting out. There had been strangers before at Janet's teas. This man was out of place, but he was certainly not offensive. He wore a tasteless gray suit and his voice, when it occasionally traveled the room to her, was subdued and of easy authority. He was too masculine for his company, yet he was refined; neither a bore nor a pusher. There was undoubtedly some scandal....

She looked at him again, at the soaring size of the man seated across the room, and wondered. Then he looked at her. And she knew that she had been looking at him from her straight-back chair since the moment she had sat down. And she knew he had been looking back. She hadn't even realized what she had been doing.

It was the nearest thing Carlotta Ford ever felt to panic. Nervously, she turned and found the eyes of her hostess inexplicably glaring at her. Suddenly, she knew everything in swift realization, why everyone was afraid. Everyone in the room except the big man.

Janet tore her gaze away from the girl and cast her hostile eyes busily about the room, following the movement of the two pert aides who worked under Diane's supervision. In majordomo style, Diane stood silently beside her mistress. The girl had been her employee for six years; at the time of their first meeting, she had been a smart and graceful girl of twenty-four. They now shared a comfortable understanding of the meaning behind these Sunday teas. The tea ritual was all about Vicki. Thinking of her daughter, Janet felt satisfied with the plans she had for the girl who was coming home the next day. Unable to contain this happy thought, she said to her maid, "I can't wait for Vicki."

Diane smiled. "How long will Miss Vicki be staying, ma'am?"

That was irritating. Diane meant (Janet thought) how long could Vicki be expected to stay without getting them involved with every predatory man in Greenville, necessitating her leaving town once again. Sometimes a little knowledge was a dangerous thing.

"Mr. Lance will be happy to see his sister," Diane offered in an effort at conciliation.

"And I," Janet added with suppressed excitement. "And all the girls too—Carlotta, Nelly—"

"Nelly?" The maid flushed. "I think Nelly is more concerned with your son."

"What was that you said, Diane?"

"I'm sorry, ma'am. I thought it was my duty—"

"Your duty to what?" her employer snapped.

The girl had certainly dragged in that "duty" business like it was something she'd rehearsed.

"Well, it's no secret that Nelly Pratt is in love with your son. Anyone can see that, Mrs. Harper."

"So what? You think I don't know the obvious? I've always known it."

Diane shrugged. "Then I'm sorry I brought it up. If you'll excuse me, I'll have someone attend to Miss Vicki's room."

"Hold on. You can do that anytime. Now, Diane, what was the reason for your statement? Do you know something I don't know? Besides the obvious fact that Nelly has a crush on Lance, which has been common knowledge since she was twelve. Has Lance taken advantage of her?"

"Not that I can see, ma'am."

Janet made a sweeping motion with her bracelet-laden wrist. "No, of course not. He wouldn't spit…. Oh, Diane, do you seriously?" She shook her head. "That girl is not only beneath him in every social sense, but she's stupid and unbearably ugly. He wouldn't notice her any sooner than he'd notice an ambitious housemaid. Do you know what I mean?"

Diane's face turned crimson. "I merely thought it my duty to bring the matter to your attention," she said stiffly. "Sometimes, young men don't know how to defend themselves."

"Especially if they're drunkards?"

"I merely said—"

"I know what you said," Janet Harper stated between clenched teeth. "But my son is not going to be trapped by any scheming bitch. Not by you and not by Nelly. He'll marry a proper girl for his station. I'll show you how Lance can defend himself. I'll show you. Clear up some dishes meanwhile and just watch."

Janet glanced across the room and noted the activity that was transpiring in Lance's boisterous group. The young men were making a big thing of sneaking the liquor into their teacups. She made her way to where Nelly was seated, wallflower-fashion, against the wall. The girl was covertly watching what Lance's group was doing.

"Don't pay attention to it, Nelly," she said kindly.

The girl remained in confused silence. A course of action was never quite clear to her with regard to Mrs. Harper. Sometimes it seemed the woman liked her; at other times, she was stormily unpredictable and unfriendly. Most often, it proved wise to say nothing when spoken to. But when Lance was like this, anxiety seized the girl, an uneasiness she understood no better than she understood most things, and she found that she had to speak to someone. Her uneasiness was, in actuality, a well-founded fear of ridicule.

The young men surrounding Lance were smiling and whispering fatuously, pleased with themselves to the point of excruciation, draped as they were over lounge, chair and table. Nelly shivered with apprehension as Janet spoke to her.

"If it bothers you, then stop looking at them," she advised the girl calmly.

Nelly dropped her stare to the large, freckled hands in her lap. She felt the woman's touch lightly on her sleeve. She looked up, almost with fright.

"But what can I do?" asked Janet plaintively. "What's the good of looking and seeing? It only draws attention to them. I could certainly forbid their coming to the parties, yes. But Lance wouldn't come if they didn't come, all his friends. And where would he go? At least here, I can keep an eye on him."

Nelly nodded uncomfortably. There was no end to the woman's moods. Though lacking insight into their meanings, Nelly had learned better than to actively participate in Mrs. Harper's moments of martyrdom lest she be left holding the mood long after the woman had herself deserted it.

In true form, the older woman was suddenly smiling, glints of sentimentality filling her blue eyes.

"It's really funny, Nelly. Here you are, hoping that Lance will sober up long enough to be civil to you or fall in love with you, and here I am, wishing he'd learn to be a more presentable son and stop disgracing me. Here are two sober women against one intoxicated man, and we can't do a damned thing."

Nelly felt faint, as she always did when her fondness for Lance was mentioned. Yet her gullible heart caught the mood of self-pity that Janet had struck for her. Often, as happened now, Nelly wondered what would happen if she were to suddenly leave, to disappear from Greenville. Mrs. Harper would certainly be at a loss. She never exposed any other girl to her innermost thoughts this way. There would be no one to share her frustrations about Lance. And Lance?

Yes, he would miss her! He would miss having someone to tease; he would find after a while that a certain spice had gone from his life. And he would one day realize that he, Lance Harper, was really in love with a girl he had never taken seriously.

"Hey, what are you thinking?" Janet leaned forward to peer into Nelly's face. "You looked so fierce there for a moment. What goes on in that head of yours that can be so fierce?"

"I'd like to spank him," whispered Nelly recklessly.

Janet chuckled. "Go ahead then. You have my permission. I'd treasure the scene to my dying day. Imagine you spanking the heir to the Harpers' millions!"

Nelly glanced across at the man of her affections. She saw that his light-colored hair caught some of the radiance of the sun that entered through the high windows. His nose was thin, somewhat bony (though straight), bespeaking a sensitiveness to her that was more than just the high-strung sensitiveness of a spoiled child. She knew that there was a certain fineness inside him.

"Come," Janet said brightly, pulling Nelly with her by the hand. "Let's start collecting dishes."

The chore always humiliated Nelly. She had to remind herself that Mrs. Harper was not above playing the part of the maid in the hope that, she'd once confided, she gave an air of intimacy to the teas, like a humble housewife in a humble home. As she entered self-consciously into groups of girls and men, Nelly waved courteously and nodded faint greetings, keeping her lips firmly over her protruding teeth.

A loud guffaw reminded her that she was approaching Lance's group. Despairingly, she realized that Mrs. Harper had neglected that corner of the room and had left it for her. She could not, she simply could not do it; not with them so drunk. She turned as if to run. Janet stood behind her, halting her with a stare.

"Go ahead, Nelly. Stop being silly. Take their dishes."

"Mrs. Harper, you know I—"

Some of the girls turned to look at her. They understood what Nelly's situation was; it was not the first time she had decided that the boys' taunts were too much for her.

"Please, Mrs. Harper," she whispered.

The hostess looked at her as though to say she was being unreasonable. Nelly felt numb and unreal and trapped. Her ruffled collar seemed much too tight around her neck. She would not—she would not obey. She brushed blindly past Janet, mumbling, "I have to drop these dishes off...."

Seeking the sanctuary of the kitchen, she thought she could hear one of the girls inside giggling, and she blushed with shame. She placed a few cups and saucers from the tray gently into the sink and pressed her sweating hands on the cold porcelain.

"Now what is this?" Janet asked reproachfully from behind her.

The girl turned with tears in her eyes. "Don't make me do it," she pleaded.

"Nelly, I don't understand you. You can't run away from things like this. You'll be the laughingstock of the town. Now go back in there."

"But you know what the boys will do!" Nelly cried. "They'll roar at me and make jokes!"

"But you *love* Lance, don't you?"

The girl stared stupidly.

"You love my son, don't you?" Janet repeated.

Was it possible that Lance's mother was on her side?

"Yes," she whispered softly.

"Well, it's no secret," Janet said. "You didn't think it was. Then you can't just keep running away from him, can you, not if you love him?"

"You want to help me?"

The girl's face was so suffused with gratitude that Janet looked up at the ceiling. "Of course, Nelly. Why, there's nothing wrong with you. You're a sweet thing. I've been thinking, just this morning, in fact, that you wouldn't make a bad wife at all for Lance. But I can't very well tell my son to marry you, can I? He's a man and a proud one, and men are funny about deciding whom they want to marry. You've got to win him yourself, young lady. Yes, I've been thinking about it, even in church this morning."

"You mean you want me to marry Lance?" the girl asked in disbelief.

"I mean that the best thing that could happen to Lance is to have a woman who loves him and who would care for him."

"I'll go out," Nelly blurted. "I don't know—I don't know what—how—"

"As I was saying," Janet broke in, "there's nothing I can do to help you. But there is something."

"Yes?"

"I can give you some help, I think. As one woman to another."

"Oh."

"For instance, why don't you ever smile?"

The girl lowered her head. "My teeth...."

"They're a little protruding, of course. But there's no reason to sacrifice your smile. In fact, Nelly, what you should do is smile more than anybody else. Seriously. Your attempt to hide your teeth only attracts attention to the fact that they do protrude a little bit. It shows how you think you look."

This was complicated for Nelly, but she was human enough to agree with the logic of someone who wanted to help her.

"Now, when you go out there, smile," Janet said energetically. "Smile with all you've got, Nelly. I'll bet my son has never even seen you smile."

"Not really."

"Come." The woman led her back into the music room. "Let's see your new personality in action."

Nelly bit her lip and fiercely eyed the noisy group of men surrounding Lance. She realized she was being gently pushed and made herself move across the room before anyone observed the prodding.

None of the men had as yet noticed her approach, but her own senses were alerted to such a degree that she could smell the whiskey long before she was near enough to attract their attention.

The face of Harry Giles was one of astonishment as, without a moment's warning, Nelly lifted a half-empty cup of cool liquid from his fingers.

"Closing time, boys," Nelly said coyly.

The others fell silent. With exaggerated gestures of politeness, they finished their cups, one gulp apiece, and handed them to her.

Now, she thought.

Careful not to drop any of the cups that balanced like towers on her small tray, Nelly bent her head toward Lance. He stared up at her with complete disbelief at her behavior.

What does he think I'm going to do, she wondered, *kiss him?* It was a funny thought. And with one's head full of funny thoughts, it was easy to smile. So she smiled.

Not six inches from Lance's horrified face, she smiled as broadly as her lips could stretch, and all the faces staring back at her were blurred because her eyes almost closed with the bigness of her smile.

It started as someone's exclamation—"Oh, God!"—and it became an avalanche of masculine laughter. Lance was laughing to the point of breathlessness; he was weak from laughter; tears rolled out of his intoxicated eyes.

"Nelly, please do that again!" he cried. "Please do it again!"

"What a beautiful, beautiful horseface!" someone else roared.

Lance, slapping his friends' knees, entreated her, "Nelly, come back here and make another horseface for my guests!" He rose majestically from his seat. "I insist, Nelly. Come back here and—"

His own sobbing laughter cut off the rest of his words. Nelly had already backed away and a low murmur of feminine tittering followed her across the room. Janet Harper stood by the door that led to the kitchen, her head thrown back, her hands on her hips. What seemed an echo of Lance's laughter rippled from her thin lips.

Only Carlotta, it seemed to Nelly, and the big man who had been at her boarding house last night—only they seemed not to have joined in the fun. The big man was frowning his disapproval, Nelly saw at a glimpse. It didn't help much, but it helped a little.

Still carrying her tray, Nelly made her way, slower now, past Janet, into the kitchen, then, after placing the dishes in the sink, out the side door. Someone followed. It was Diane, the maid.

Nelly was in tears as Diane took her arm. "Let's just walk around the grounds," the maid said kindly. "I can't go very far. I have to clean up after the mob leaves, and I've only got a few minutes. Come on. Hurry."

"I'm a fool. A fool!" said Nelly, allowing herself to be prodded along, "What can I do when I just love him?"

"That's not enough," said Diane as they entered the driveway where the guests' cars were haphazardly parked. "If every girl got the man she loved—"

Nelly broke into tears again as the picture of Lance's hilarity rose anew to sicken her. The maid gripped her shoulder.

"Stop thinking about it."

"I can't take it anymore, Diane. Boys always teased me. In school, they—sometimes I thought they were trying to get even with me for something."

"Maybe they were. Maybe you wouldn't give them the one thing they wanted, Nelly."

"But I would. I'd give Lance anything if he asked me."

"Anything?" the maid asked.

Harriet Simms and Nancy Crowell came out of the building and walked by on the way to their cars. "Out for a walk?" Harriet asked, frowning briefly at Diane. Nelly was still formulating an answer when the girls were already out of earshot.

"Don't bother," Diane said, "they can't hear you. That's what you get for walking outside when you're the hired help. You do this often enough and you'll get an interesting reputation. And who knows? It may be just the thing to get Lance interested in you." She laughed mirthlessly. "Nelly— the girl who rebelled against her class. But then again, you aren't really in their class, are you? Your mother runs a boarding house. You're just an interloper like me, after all."

"Class? I don't think anyone cares about that."

"Maybe not. Skip it. Let's get back to the subject."

"Forget it, Diane. I know what you mean, and I wouldn't—I just couldn't do that."

"Well, it's up to you." The taller girl shrugged. "Just giving you some free advice. To put it bluntly, a girl can win a man by letting him have his way with her. At least he'd notice her then. Usually, they ask you to marry them afterwards. If a girl's in love, it's not really much of a sacrifice, is it? Most girls your age today aren't virgins, you know."

"I realize that. Are you?"

"Of course not. I'm a little older than you, and I'm not from a small town. I got my man that way, too. It so happens he was killed in Vietnam. But I don't want to talk about that. One thing I don't regret is what I did with that man." She turned abruptly to walk toward the house. "I have to go back now."

"But how—?" Nelly started.

"We'll have to talk some more. Come around later this afternoon," Diane suggested. "Ask the cook to call me down. Then we'll figure out how to arrange it."

"All right." Nelly nodded. "I'll be here, promise."

Inside the music room, Carlotta watched as Mildred approached. The tall, skinny girl often did social chores for Janet exactly the way Nelly did, and it was not unusual to receive a summons from either one of them. Suddenly, Mildred was standing awkwardly above her.

"Mrs. Harper wants to see you in the kitchen, Carl."

Carlotta looked around the room. Many of the guests had gone, but some remained, talking animatedly, singing around the piano. Janet had indeed disappeared.

"Thank you, Milly," she said, not looking at the girl.

Making her way unhurriedly across the room, she knew that the big man, who sat on a couch between two Jefferson girls, was watching her body; she could feel his eyes on her back. With a mental shrug, she forgot him entirely, and she smiled and shook her head regretfully at the group of girls around the piano who beckoned her to join them.

In the kitchen, the hostess was staring restlessly from the window at the hills of lawn that surrounded her estate. She did not turn as Carlotta entered. The girl waited respectfully, studying the woman's narrow back, watching the light of the window create a cruel halo of the absurd blonde-white hair that spoke of too many treatments and too little taste. She smiled inwardly at the familiar clawlike gesture of the woman's ringed fingers and the nervous jangling of the bracelets that climbed up and down Janet's left arm. Then Carlotta stopped smiling and thought, as she so often did, in renewed wonder: this woman owns every important newspaper in the state. This woman sells soda pop to almost every country in the world. This is the woman who, when her husband died over fifteen years ago, had not retired into quiet young widowhood or remarried but who expanded, in one generation, the business that her husband's family had built over many generations, expanded the town and the business to an unbelievable degree. Janet was no more a successor; she was an innovator. And it was tragic to think that some day, Lance and Vicki would succeed her.

"Hello, Carlotta," Janet said, swinging about to face her. There was something obscene about the thin, powdered face, the ready smile, the suggestion of crow's feet around the deadly blue eyes. "Enjoying yourself?"

"Yes, of course, Mrs. Harper."

The woman's eyes searched the girl's face for a flickering moment. The red-painted mouth twisted suddenly at some private conclusion.

"Carl...this is Morrison."

"Morrison?"

"The tall man. I want you—" The mouth twisted again, violently this time, as though unable to find words for itself.

"Yes?"

"To stay away from him."

For an instant, she was too surprised to answer. Mrs. Harper then commenced to walk around her, looking her up and down as if she were for sale. Carlotta was dumbfounded.

"Be cordial, of course," the woman instructed her. "But no more than usual."

I haven't exchanged a single word with that man, Carlotta wanted to say. But she could never say that because she had never learned or believed in the necessity of explaining herself, even when she was misunderstood.

"Why," she asked, "should I stay away from him?"

"How's your mother, Carlotta?"

"She's well, thank you," came the stiff response.

"Is that all she is?"

"What?!" cried Carlotta before she could stop herself. Then her beautiful face paled with rage, for she knew that Janet was threatening her.

She knew that Janet wanted her to say, if only to herself, My mother is grateful because she was elected president of the garden club last April. My mother knows, of course, that it is you who decide elections around here. And the rest of it: My father—for his job, his social position in Greenville. Myself—for you've nurtured me along with your own daughter; for you've seen to it that I've always belonged and that my family has always belonged. And although you can take all of this away from us in one day, you have never thought of doing so. For that, we are thankful.

But Carlotta Ford, who had grown up proud, could never say any of this.

"I'm going home now," she said quite abruptly. "You'll forgive me, I'm sure."

A cold hand detained her.

"No, I want you to stay. It would look very odd if you left after coming in here. So you'll stay. It's quite apparent that he's taken an interest in you. He's been staring at you and asking your name, and you've been staring back. Not that I blame either one of you. But you can't leave now and have it appear to others that I'm afraid of the prettiest girl in town." She paused to glare at the girl. "Stay awhile. And I think I'd also want you to accept every invitation I arrange in the next few weeks. There will be a lot of parties and things to celebrate Vicki's homecoming. You're Vicki's best friend, after all, and it would certainly be noticed if you chose to be absent. So we'll be seeing a lot of each other, I hope."

Carlotta, her mouth dry, nodded distantly.

"I understand. And how long will your Mr. Morrison be in Greenville?"

She had stressed the possessive pronoun faintly and watched Janet Harper brazenly. The older woman's face turned an angry red as she stared Carlotta down.

"He's not *my* Mr. Morrison," she hissed. "I could slap your face for saying that."

Carlotta smiled, unreasonably sure of herself once more, and her voice was soft and husky. "I didn't believe he was. But he must be someone's. Can I assume he's Vicki's?"

"Yes," Janet said, not blinking an eye, "he's Vicki's."

The dark-haired girl shrugged. Actually, she didn't care. But she did wonder why the widow should find a man for Vicki and not for herself. In a way, she understood. Something did have to be done about that girl. And about Lance as well. Incidents involving Vicki and Lance crowded in on her memory, unwanted, that Carlotta *did* care about inasmuch as they comprised her own history:

The private school in Jefferson, a brown, musty building. She and Vicki and the older Lance, already in high school, waiting for the chauffeur to take them to their respective schools. The slum boy, Bart, who came to make fun of Lance, then Lance's running away. Vicki's laughter because her brother was so much taller than Bart.

"Coward!" Janet had cried at Lance.

The flat-nosed teacher, the boxing gloves, the punching bag in the summer cottage. The running away again. Again and again. The investigation of the family of a slum boy, a bully, who never stopped taunting the rich boy. The slum boy's father's sudden achievement of success in the Harper factories. The boy himself, Bart Seely, now an important man. Lance must always be reminded of his cowardice. He must never be allowed to become a man in his own right. The widow encouraging her son to drink. The widow who wanted her son to stay with her. The desperate rich boy who rode freights, who tried again and again to escape, but who came home always....

And Vicki at fifteen, who rebelled against the chauffeur and the rigidity of coming and going. The late afternoons, Vicki and Carlotta. Older Lance already drinking elsewhere. She and Vicki in Jefferson's streets and stores. Vicki stealing small and senseless things. The irate shopkeepers reporting to the widow.

"Thief!" Janet had cried at Vicki.

The jewelry ordered for Vicki, the New York and Paris dresses. The car. The spoiling that erased all character. The dependence on the money. The terrible dependence.

And the countermeasures. The Sunday tea ritual for the young people so that the right ones were near Vicki. The double-dating in Vicki's car.

"Stay near her, Carlotta," Janet had said. "She doesn't know how to freeze a boy the way you can."

Carlotta, the cold one, the safe one, the wet blanket, the icy beauty. While, in the front seat, the bold necking and more than that.

The restless, thrill-seeking Vicki. The trips to the aunt in Boston or the aunt in New Orleans, neither of whom existed. The hurried trips away from Greenville, away from the men—factory workers, city slicker transients, loafers—who made the fabulous conquest. The slow removal of the men who were not transients and who would not forget the conquest.

Yes, Carlotta thought now, as she looked at the determined lips of the woman before her—he's Vicki's. He's been inspected, bottled and is ready to be capped. But why, really?

"Why is he so important?" she asked frankly. "Why do you have to choose a man for Vicki? She can find her own soon enough."

"Why him?" The older woman chuckled with surprise at the girl's obtuseness. "Really. You don't know why?"

It's because he's a man, Carlotta thought, a real man, one whom Janet Harper, most critical of judges, really considered a man. Perhaps a man who could keep Vicki home. And she was right about his being a man. Not only in size but in a certain inner strength. It showed. She had seen it herself, and she had been drawn to it despite herself. Had it needed Janet's opinion for Carlotta to know it?

"Yes, I know why," she said softly.

The woman snorted. "Well, I was hoping for your sake that you didn't. It would be less difficult for you."

"There are many such men," said Carlotta.

"Of course." The woman was laughing at her lie.

"When is Vicki coming home?"

"The day after tomorrow. She's arriving by plane."

"I see." What Carlotta saw was that Janet hoped her daughter would never want to leave again. There was something pitiful about the whole thing.

"How did you enjoy the tea?" asked the hostess.

Carlotta's lovely lips quirked. "You mean Nelly's baptism by fire?"

"You must admit," Janet said good-humoredly, "that it's terribly presumptuous of the girl. A Harper deserves someone with more beauty and poise. Someone, in fact, like you, Carlotta. I'd never object to someone like you. I've always considered you as a second daughter anyway."

Carlotta became frightened again at the thought of the woman's real power. But the idea just as quickly became ludicrous. With a suddenness that surprised both of them, she burst into laughter at the very idea of being married to Lance. Janet's shocked expression did not cut short Carlotta's mirth.

"Let's hope your little boy finds a beautiful and poised girl who looks just like me, then," Carlotta said when she finally stopped laughing.

Then, without another word, she walked beautifully from the room.

The music room was virtually empty; it was not necessary to carry out the hostess's instructions about remaining. She found her light coat and went to find her car. Nelly was waiting there for her.

"I've been wanting to talk to you. Thanks, Carl, for not laughing at me," the girl said breathlessly.

"Of course I wouldn't laugh at you."

"Carl, tell me something."

Carlotta waited for the girl to continue, her hand on the car door. She was impatient to be off, away from this place of recent humiliations...but she was fond of Nelly, and the girl's fumbling inability to cope with the mysteries of human relationships had not made her less fond through their growing-up years. She waited without much interest and without prompting for the girl to ask her momentous question. Nelly was blushing through her freckles.

"IF you wanted something—" the homely girl started. "If you loved...well, do you think a girl should go after what she wants? Even if other people would think it was bad? Do you?"

Carlotta knew what was on the girl's mind and was surprised. The negative answer rose instantly to her lips, but they remained closed. She still smarted from her encounter with Janet Harper. She did not like being told she was not to receive the admiration of any man. She did not like being told this by anyone.

"Yes," she whispered into Nelly's face. "Yes, if I really wanted a man, really wanted him, I wouldn't care how I got him. I'd get him somehow. And I wouldn't let anyone on earth tell me I wasn't to have that man or wasn't going to get him any way I could. It so happens...." Her voice became calm. "It so happens that I don't love any man that much.

But if I did, Nelly dear, I assure you that no one would tell me I couldn't have him. I wouldn't care what anyone in this town thought, not even the powers that be. Do you understand me?"

Nelly nodded, evidently flabbergasted by Carlotta's uncharacteristic intensity. Had she been less personally disturbed, Carlotta might have found amusement in the effect of her outburst.

"Thanks," Nelly said. "That's all I wanted to know. Will you give me a lift home?"

Carlotta drove her to the boarding house. As she watched Nelly climb the steps, she had a moment of regret, a longing to call her back. She knew what Nelly was thinking, although she doubted that the girl would go through with her intentions or that it would ever go beyond the fantasy stage. But she didn't care if it did. She remembered Janet Harper's insinuation of a possible future between Lance and herself, and she didn't care at all what Nelly Pratt had in mind for Lance Harper.

You're a compulsive. That doesn't mean you have constant compulsions to do things; it means you hold onto yourself for dear life, you refuse to lose control. So you cannot feel.

And what is the emotion you're most afraid of? Do you think it's love? Or fear or hate? I don't think it's any of those things. I believe you're afraid of wonder, of awe, of bigness. There is certainly nothing more awesome and full of wonder than a female of the species. But you're afraid of that wonderment because it's symphonic and universal and too grand to contemplate. You're afraid to raise your manhood to the heavens.

Frankly, I don't think there is any psychoanalytic technique that can help you. For you, it's a matter of finding a new way of looking at the universe. You have to break away from yourself and start at some new place you don't recognize, that you've never even heard of. Whether this requires drugs or insanity or what I cannot say. But I think drugs would work for you, and it's a pity you refuse them. There's that matter of control again: you're afraid drugs will take away your control...and you're right. But that fear—that's the root of your problem, isn't it?

CHAPTER 3

Police Lieutenant James Schwartz leaned back in his well-worn swivel chair and blew cigar smoke into the air. He grimaced not unpleasantly as he invited Morrison to sit on the other side of his desk.

"Now, we don't mean to harass you, young fellow, and I'm sorry that I had to call you from that comfortable place you're at to come down here this morning. I know this isn't the nicest place to come to. It's nothing so grand as Mrs. Harper's." He stretched out his palms in a helpless gesture. "But I'm a servant of the people and I do what I have to do. Schwartz is the name. Now let's hear about you and Ned Amsterdam."

"Sure. What do you want to know?"

The lieutenant's dark, heavy eyebrows formed a thoughtful V shape. "I understand he gave you a lift in his car. That's harmless enough. But maybe you can help us. Did you and Amsterdam stop anywhere along the way?"

"Yes, we did. He wanted to stop for a drink. It was a place on Route 8. Blue Lagoon or something like that, it was called."

The lieutenant nodded. "How come you didn't mention that to the officers before?"

"They didn't ask me."

"Did anybody see you there?"

"The bartender."

"Anyone else?"

"I don't think so."

"Well, that's not the way we hear it. How come you're forgetting about the other people?"

Morrison fell silent.

"We know you were there," the policeman went on. "We checked all along the route up here and we spoke to the bartender. Now, he says there were two girls. Hookers. What happened with the girls, Morrison?"

"Nothing at all."

"But I understand Amsterdam was trying to pick them up. The bartender heard him talking to them. Did the girls get into the car?"

"No, they didn't leave the bar with us. He was trying to pick one of them up but changed his mind."

"You sure of that? What made him change his mind?"

"I don't know."

"You changed it for him, right, kid?"

Morrison shrugged his heavy shoulders. "Could be."

"You didn't want any part of those girls, right? Why? It's not really too important to the investigation, but when things don't fit right, I want to know the answers. Why didn't you want anything to do with the hookers?"

"I just didn't."

"But there must be a reason. Were they too ugly for you?"

"Let's just say prostitution's against the law. I didn't want to have anything to do with breaking the law."

"Yeah, we could say that." The dark eyes were frankly curious. "Or maybe you're the type that doesn't like to pay for it. There are lots of guys like that, who make it a point never to pay for it. Are you like that, Morrison?"

"You might say so."

The lieutenant was thoughtful. But he seemed to have decided to forget the subject of the girls. He stroked his chin and said, "There's something very puzzling about you, Morrison."

When Morrison didn't ask what it was, the cop went on with his thought. "It's that you don't care what happens to you. Isn't that right? You don't even care if I arrest you."

"That's not true. I don't want to get arrested."

"Maybe you don't. But I'll tell you one thing. I've had a lot of people sitting across this desk of mine, and I can tell when somebody's scared of being arrested, innocent or not. You just don't give a damn. I'm pretty sure you didn't do anything wrong, mind you. Still, I have to tell you not to leave town."

"All right, I won't."

Lieutenant Schwartz shook his head. "See what I mean? One town's as good as another to you, isn't it?"

"I'm looking for a job."

"Yeah, that's what I hear." For the first time, the lieutenant smiled broadly. "I hear you got one lulu of a job, kid. Good luck." He was still smiling when his guest walked out.

"Have we spoken about Vicki?" Janet asked brightly. "You'll meet her tomorrow at the airport, but I think I'd like to tell you about her first. You'll like her. She may seem crude at times, you can't help but think that, but now you've been warned. It's like a cover-up because she's really a person of some depth."

Morrison ate.

"Most people see the surface," Janet said tritely, hoping to imply that he was not like most people. "Some man who has strength—strength of character, I mean—could bring out the best in Vicki."

Morrison ate. Jesus wept and Morrison ate.

"Perhaps you've heard things about my daughter?" she questioned, staring all the way down the mahogany table at the busily masticating face at the other end. The dining room was the somber room in the house, with panels of worm-eaten oak and the table too long and formal. She would have it redone one of these days. Morrison was looking up at her momentarily with an expression that proclaimed innocence of having heard things about Vicki, and suddenly she felt like all kinds of an idiot. She threw her head back and laughed, scratching at her hair.

"Then it was foolish of me to say that," she admitted. "However, if you're going to be in Greenville for any length of time, then you'll hear some tales about Vicki. They're exaggerated, of course."

"You don't need to tell me," he interjected.

"But I do."

"Yeah, I guess you do."

"I have no secrets from you, Morrison, not about this family," she said.

"Guess not."

"Vicki *has* been wild. She's young. She's always been young, even when she was a child. That sounds stupid, but do you understand what I mean?"

He nodded.

"She believed, I think, that it was her duty to desecrate herself, her respectability. She has spirit. She makes a point of being unconventional, that's all it is. There were many boyfriends. She played with them the way some girls play with dolls. It meant nothing. A doll means nothing. Well, neither did the boys. She never fell in love, even if she thought she did once or twice. You understand all this?"

"I understand," he said, putting the finishing touches to his plate of turkey and salad. "I understand that you're a very devoted mother and you love your children and you look beneath the surface to their good selves."

She blinked at him. "Are you putting me on?"

"Yes, actually, I am."

"Don't do that, please."

"All right. You've got your troubles, I think."

She held back the tears that were threatening to spill out. It was very easy for her to give way to a martyred feeling of self-appreciation. She did this often in the privacy of her room. But she sensed that Morrison would look upon it darkly.

"I do indeed have my troubles," she said, inexplicably gaily. "My children...I want them home with me. I look forward to the day when they're both married. I'll give one of them this house or I'll build homes for them nearby."

"In Greenville?"

"What? You disapprove? Well, it doesn't have to be right in town. But I'm a lonely woman. Lance came home just a few days ago...traveling around the country. Vicki's been away almost a year. Now they'll both be back with me. I don't intend to let them go away again. I want them to settle down. Lance could take over some of the responsibilities of the company. Believe it or not, he's quite intelligent. Vicki could marry, and her husband could also take a responsible position.... Well, that's besides the point. But this time, I've made up my mind that they're going to settle down and become a part of things in this town where they belong. So far, Vicki hasn't found any man who's suitable, and Lance hasn't found a girl interesting enough. You can understand how I feel, right?"

He sat like a rock. She could see him weighing everything she said. She realized she'd been rather blunt about his role and she cursed herself. She needed to learn to use subtlety with this man. Having been a big fish in her small pond for so long, one lost the art of subtlety; one became a tyrant. Morrison seemed to have receded from her. Indeed, where a moment ago his elbows had been familiarly planted at the edge of the table, he was now seated upright in his chair. He had, it seemed, understood all too well everything she said. She smiled.

"Listen to the mother!" she said with a smile. "I suppose my children will find their own mates in good time, won't they? I'm much too clever to interfere. You know that, don't you?"

"I'm sure you are," he affirmed.

They finished the meal and the maid brought coffee. When she left, Morrison leaned forward.

"This girl Carlotta Ford," he said. "She's very beautiful."

"Who?"

"I wonder how it is she's not married."

"Carlotta?" Janet chuckled, although she was annoyed that he talked on despite her pretense of not hearing the name. "So you found out who she is. Forget her. She's a very cold girl."

"Cold?"

"A girl of good character. In fact, it was for that reason I threw her together with Vicki. My purpose was to keep Vicki's spirit under a cold faucet so she wouldn't run away with herself. Carlotta," she said, "is just such a cold faucet."

"Pity, seeing as she's so beautiful. Are you sure?"

"Why would I say so if I wasn't sure? Anyone will tell you the same thing."

He nodded. "Oh, I believe you. I don't need to ask anyone else."

That seemed to be enough for him. She wondered at having dispensed with Carlotta so easily. Yet a vague feeling persisted that Morrison was somehow pleased to learn of the girl's coldness.

Lance entered the room before she had the time to analyze this disquieting thought. Her son stared suspiciously at the big man, who, seemingly in excellent humor now, rose to say he was going to take a stroll around the estate. Lance slid into the abandoned chair when Morrison got up, taking up less than half the space. The maid entered and Lance signaled her to clear the dishes in front of him. Janet put a cigarette to her lips and the girl jumped to light it for her.

"Mother," said Lance when the maid finally retired. "I didn't have a chance to ask you yesterday. Who is this big oaf?"

"Someone I just hired, dear."

"For what? Do you want me to take boxing lessons again at my age? Or will it be wrestling this time?"

"Don't be silly. He'll do all sorts of things. Chauffeur, for instance."

"You're being very strange about him, Mother, I must say. What's wrong with the chauffeur we have? Old William, I mean. How come the big ox is at your tea party, charming all my friends and all the ladies, and here having lunch in my seat?"

She flushed in annoyance at his possessive pride.

"Mother! Don't tell me—at your age! Why, you're blushing!"

She cut him off with an angry glance. "Don't be an ass. It's not for me."

Lance's mouth dropped to make his face the complete picture of bewilderment. Then a knowing look transformed his features.

"Just when Vicki's coming home!"

When his mother assented coldly to the truth of his discovery, he went on to say, "I don't get it. And what I do get sounds awful."

"Why awful?" his mother snapped. "I want Vicki home. I want her home for good, if possible. If there's a man around the house who'll keep her entertained...."

She let her voice fall off, and Lance swallowed as if he had tasted something he didn't like.

"This is morbid, Mother," he said hoarsely. "What the hell kind of place are you running here?"

"Watch your tongue!" she hissed. "Since when is sex such a subject of disgust in this house? You know very well that Vicki can't control herself. I mean that literally. She cannot control her urges."

"So?"

"I made a simple arrangement, that's all," she whispered to her son's pale face.

"Since when did you begin to get men for Vicki?"

"Since now. I want you both home. I miss you when you're not here, whether you realize it or not. I don't want you and Vicki running around the world anymore, writing home for money, visiting once a year. This time, I've made up my mind. Home is the place for both of you. That means you, too. You can stay drunk here as well as anyplace else in the world. And this way, bums and hoboes won't get their hands on your money either."

"All right, all right. But if we stay home, we can get our own—I can get my own women and Vicki can get her own men. She damn well can."

Janet silenced his outburst with a quick gesture of her hand. "No, that's out for Vicki. No more chasing around with every pair of pants in this town. I've got to live here. And from now on, so do you and so does she. And so do your children. It's a simple matter of sex. And do you think I'm going to let sex keep this family apart forever? Sex drives you both away. Vicki, because she makes me send her away or I'd never be able to walk through the streets with my head up and all the boys snickering at me about my daughter. And you, too," she added, glancing sadly at him, her voice dropping. "That's why you drink. Because you're not sure how much of a man you are. You let those hoboes do all kinds of things to you, don't you?"

All the blood drained from his face. "You don't have to insult me, Mother," he said softly.

She raised a hand weakly as though to touch him, stopping short of contact. "I'm sorry, Lance."

"Who says...what makes you think—"

"I didn't mean what I said, dear. Forget it, please. I got so used to hearing about you running away from fights. But actually, that's not the right way to judge a man."

He thought about this. "Well, it'll do until another way comes along," he admitted sadly. "But sometimes I think you don't want me to be a man at all."

"Don't be silly. Now, this man for Vicki—his name is Morrison. If anyone asks you who he is, say he's a companion for you. Like you said before, to teach you boxing."

"That's no good, Mother. I'm too old for that crap."

"Then say he's a friend. Until we know what Vicki thinks of him, we'll play it that way. And don't hate him. He's just another man, after all, and Vicki's had plenty. So there's no reason to object to one more, is there?"

"But it's mighty peculiar, a girl's own mother arranging a thing like this."

"It's not peculiar at all. It's just about time I started arranging things in my own family."

"But I just can't—"

"You don't have to," she told him icily. "You're never to breathe a word of this arrangement to anyone, do you understand that, Lance? Remember that. Even when you're in your cups. Just keep the fact in front of your mind that you must never mention it. It won't be a secret forever if Vicki likes him—if she does like him. But until it's settled one way or another, I don't want you and your cronies talking about it. If you do babble about this, you may not have your cronies for very long."

He didn't answer. She could see that he knew what she meant: that she could cut off his allowance and his liquor supply.

She was satisfied that he really didn't care much about Vicki, anyway. As long as he had his bottle. She could probably tell him which girl to marry and he would do it without a battle, just as long as the liquor held out.

"You better eat," she said. "Get some food in your stomach so you can hold your liquor tonight. You're going to Timothy's Bar, I have no doubt."

He didn't deny it.

Your mother is long dead, but we've got to meet her because this time you're going to fuck her, fuck her to death. Let's go, up to heaven. A little psychodrama now. Evelyn, you play his mother, come on, come on, say hello my darling son.... You've got to act this out, Morrison, or you'll never get free of it. Get on top of her. So what if nothing's happening. Pretend it is. Pretend your dick is sticking into her. Ah, that's it. Up, down, shove it in. I know you're very strong but if you shove it into a woman, it doesn't kill her. A vagina's the least delicate and least virginal place on earth. So if you're afraid to hurt a woman, forget it. They love to be hurt. Go ahead, shove in a couple of fingers. There, see, she loves it. Remember now, she's your mother....

CHAPTER 4

That afternoon, Bart Seely was seated in his office, feet up on his desk, when suddenly the terror came over him. It came out of nowhere. He had just hung up the telephone after dunning a poor sap who was behind on his car payments. He scared the wits out of this young stuttering man with the threat not only of repossession but also hints at charges of fraud and other wrongdoing. It was old stuff for Bart, and the sense of uneasiness he'd begun to experience during the conversation obviously could have nothing to do with the content of their discussion.

It was something in the young man's voice, a lisping, whining quality, that had set off the unaccountable echoes of his own thoughts. Pictures of the youngster's hairless face and smooth-bodied countenance drifted across his consciousness, a day-dreaming appreciation of imagined comeliness. By the end of what was essentially a routine business conversation, Bart was drenched with perspiration and literally chattering as he uttered his last threat. His heart was pounding fiercely as though it had grown to twice its size.

Leaping from his chair, Bart hurried past his startled secretary with a hoarse cry about returning later. He made his way on the edge of panic to Eddie's. There, half-standing and one leg over the barstool, he quickly downed two straight shots and waited for his trembling to stop. As he gained control of himself, he thought, *This isn't the first time.* Lately, his dreams had been sending him off into terrified wakefulness at ungodly hours of the night. He had also felt this way after beating up the big man.

Bart knew what this was all about. The dreams were explicit enough, and the big man's Greek god body had sent out the same signals. What was happening to him? He was a grown man. He had always been normal. There was nothing more disgusting to him than a mincing.... He wouldn't even think of the word to describe what he was calling himself.

He ordered another drink. Christ, he couldn't even look the bartender in the eye.

★★★

She and Nelly had come very late and yet were waiting more than an hour. She watched, crouching in the bush, an unlit flashlight dangling from one hand, the other hand gripping the arm of the trembling girl. As they waited, she looked around in the dusk. Shrubs, flowers and moss were to be seen in patches, barely signs of nature. Hardy shrubs gave covering but no beauty. Everywhere along the tracks was a stamp of abandonment and loneliness.

She watched with impatience as one house light after another went out. The people on this side of the tracks, hard-working like her own parents back East, were going to bed early because they wanted, she was sure, to be healthy, wealthy and wise.

Her gaze fastened once again on the open doorway of Timothy's Bar, at the light spilling palely into the dark, quiet street. Occasionally, a figure sauntered down the street into the bar; occasionally men came out. From inside Timothy's filtered the guffaws of the young and the old, the violent sound of masculine aggressiveness that thrilled her not at all. She was by no means a fool, as was this girl crouching beside her, and she would use a man but never be used by one.

It would all go well, thought Diane, because Nelly was ready for tonight, ready to become Janet's enemy. What the stupid girl could never understand was that Janet's love for her son would not allow for his body or his heart to be won by any other woman. She would choose the woman who was to be Lance's wife and she would choose someone who didn't try to love Lance or compete. One must not try to win Lance; one must win his mother.

Of course, in the long run, Nelly could have won out. The girl loved Lance, but with so patient a love that it was not like love at all, just something to do...certainly not offensive to the mother, no more offensive than the ambitions of a maid. Nelly stood as good a chance as Diane of receiving Janet's blessings—and the Harper prestige. The girl, in her stupidity, could never win Lance away from his mother anyway.

But today, it could be changed. The mother could be offended by the simpleminded one. The mother could indeed be frightened by the sexual weapon wielded by the simpleminded one. A disinterested maid, one who knew her place as secondary, could answer everyone's problems.

There was a silence in Timothy's as though all within were listening to the narration of a story. Then came, as it had to come, the burst of laughter. A good joke, thought Diane, a good male joke, and maybe it was about a woman who wanted a man so much that she seduced him while he was drunk. That would make men laugh, wouldn't it?

"He'll be coming out soon, I think," she offered the trembling girl beside her. And indeed the door of the bar filled with shadows as five or six men emerged.

She hushed Nelly's forthcoming comment and raked the group with her squinting eyes. "I can't tell. Is he with them?"

Nelly's dress rustled in the darkness. "He's there. I can't see much either, but I can tell by his walk."

Of course you'd know his walk, you fool.

The men were near them, staggering by.

"We've got to get him away from the others," Diane whispered.

Nelly rustled again. "I don't see how. He's very drunk. He's the only one who is really drunk. One of them is holding him up. Oh no, I don't see how—not unless I go out and tell them I'm going to take him home."

Diane grunted. *They might not let you, darling,* she thought. "No," she said thoughtfully. "I'll get rid of them. There's one way to make a pack of rats scamper for the hills." She stood up tall, much to the relief of all her cramped muscles, and brushed at her dress. "You stay here, Nelly. I'll come back for you."

A moment later, she was stalking the six men through several streets in the poorest, darkest section of Greenville. She waited until they were near the tracks because they were taking Lance to his side of the world after he had spent who knows how much money feeding them liquor for the privilege of their company.

As they approached the upgrade to the tracks, she turned around once more to assure herself that no one was in sight behind her. She hid from them behind a tree. Then, cupping her hands around her lips so that her voice would carry only to the men now struggling up to the tracks, she tried to simulate in her shouting the muffled voice of a woman still far away.

"Thieves! Thieves!"

In a body they turned. But they could not see her. The man holding Lance held him off slightly, ready for flight. Again she screamed, weirdly, as though only a trick of the wind carried her voice to them:

"Those men by the tracks. Those men did it. Get them, get after them!"

They ran. They threw Lance into the bushes, where he would be hidden and scattered over the rails. A few minutes of silence later, she bent laughingly over the body.

He was unconscious but unhurt; she knew he was out because of the drinking, not the fall—his head had landed safely in the bushes.

She moved him away from the place where he had fallen, back from the slope, so that if his friends returned, they would think he had gone home. She was reasonably sure, however, that they would not return. She snapped on her flashlight and rested his head carefully on the wet moss at the base of a tree and wiped the dirt from his smooth cheek. She looked at him. He had the face of a weakling, and she couldn't help but loathe him. Yet her likes and dislikes mattered little when there was so much at stake.

Nelly arrived, panting, large-eyed and trembling again. Diane wordlessly led her to the sleeping body under the sheltering tree. Both stood motionless for a moment.

"Do you want a flashlight?"

Nelly shook her head. There were tears in her eyes.

"Well, so long," Diane said briefly. "There's a moon, so you can see what you're doing. And anyway, I need the light because I don't know this end of town very well."

With a wave of her hand, she stepped quickly, attacking the upgrade, her flashlight beam bobbing before her, then disappeared over the hill.

Nelly stared for a moment into the night. She said, "Thanks," but it was too low to have been heard. She looked down at the foot of the tree. She knelt and took his face into her two hands. He groaned helplessly. For a second, he looked at her and knew vaguely where he was but not who was with him. Then he swam back and forth into unconsciousness.

He was cold and warm, tortured and soothed, his body a mouth of sensation, delicious and terrible. They were sensations: they could not be named or combined into a single experience but could be accepted only and endured, as an infant endures a mother's ministrations, with something like faith; a pagan faith, to be sure. Even pain: he knew that he was outdoors, the air sharp and cold to his nostrils; there was rock and moss and brush and twig beneath him, hurting him; but all part of a beautiful faith, abandon.

He dreamed for a moment he was on the freight again, and the bums had found him again, and they thought what they did to him and made him do could possibly despoil him. Ridiculous. He laughed aloud.

He was a schoolboy again. Bart was hitting him, sitting on top of him, hurting him, and he was crying.

No. Fingers were at his clothing. Bart would never do that.

He was a boy again, learning for the first time the clean joy of his body and lying nude in his bed to feel the air on him. He had loved contrasts, like the warm bed at the same time as the cold air on his body. Contrasts...they asked so much of you and gave back so much more. Hot drinks never so savory as with the icy night wind tightening the skin of his face while out camping with the scout troop; the dive into the creek on the sweltering day; the ravenous appetite for ice cold sodas after running in the sun all day; the pebble shaken out of the shoe; the bathed exhaustion of the big bed. He sighed.

He was a baby again, the world above him, leaning in. Someone, a perfumed someone, tending his wants, had undressed him and was warming him. Lips, he felt, breasts, he felt—a woman's body. The warmth of fondling. He was drunk and in a bush and yet he was in a crib and the breasts were upon him. The blood was pounding in his ears like a train passing and there was even the flickering light on his clouded brain of a train passing. Warmth was surging through him.

"Mother!" he cried, giving himself to the blur above. "Mother, Mother..."

Gnash your teeth, show some anger, some ecstasy. Don't be such an alienated robot. I think you're afraid of blood. It's not because you're so strong that you avoid physical horseplay with the others; it's because you don't want anyone to bleed or even to get red marks on their skin. You avoid physical contact not only because you have a sexual shyness but because you don't want to feel. Feeling is blood, the penis needs blood, and that's what you're not giving it. You should be whipped. Seriously. Go out in that world and let someone whip you. Feel the blood come in welts on your back, let yourself feel your own blood....

CHAPTER 5

She stood up tall as her plane touched the ground. She was not very tall naturally, but the nearness of Jefferson always stirred her this way, so that she was lifted, like a marionette.

It was the memory of all the fun that stirred her, body memory, which was longer than her mind memory; it was a pity that Mother was in such an unreasonable rush to have her home or else she would have spent the entire day strolling around the streets as she used to with Carlotta or have the chauffeur drive along the roads in and around Jefferson where she'd parked and made love.

It was not that she was sentimental about having at one time been a younger version of herself; it was that she respected her body and had learned to believe in it as something akin to a religion. It was this memory of nerve and muscle that had reacted so immediately to the town on alighting from the plane. Her mind, as always, seemed to follow where the body led.

The car—where was the car? The wind off the airfield roared at her back, tightening her dress to a figure that was both slender and voluptuous—in the right places, the men liked to say—as she looked around for the sedan. She sought out the longest, shiniest, chromiest car and made her way toward it, the wind almost pushing her and scattering her silky blonde curls into her eyes. She felt absolutely windswept and undressed. Oh, if she only didn't have to go directly home!

She saw that William was not in the sedan; it was empty. Suddenly, a big man, as tall and broad a man as she could ever remember seeing, stepped in front of her.

"Miss Harper?"

Vicki looked at him sharply.

"Where's William?" she asked, seeing the chauffeur's cap perched ridiculously on the big man's head. She was a girl of strange loyalties, considering that she hardly knew William at all.

"I'm driving for him this morning," he explained laconically.

She waved her fingers lightly, dismissing the subject. "Well, it doesn't really matter, does it? Walk to the car, won't you? I want to look at you from the back. Don't worry, I'll follow you. I won't run away."

She walked behind as she promised, nodding her pretty head appreciatively at his incredible physique, cursing her mother bitterly at intervals for having sent this man instead of the old geezer. Hating the new driver now, she refused to look at him as he opened the rear door for her. Numbly, she slid into her seat and fell back, closing her eyes, although she was far from tired. Slowly, expertly, he weaved the car out of the airport.

"Drive slowly," she said.

He complied, and she watched the dull landscape sweeping lazily past them.

"What's your name?" she asked.

"Morrison."

"What happened to William?"

"Nothing. He's still the chauffeur."

"That's what I figured. Why are you taking over for him this morning?"

The big shoulders heaved in a massive shrug. "Probably because he'd rather be here, so I'm here."

"Which means?"

"Which means that people don't aways get to do what they want to do."

"I don't know what you're talking about," Vicki said dryly. "That's probably why you're driving someone else's car instead of your own, because you don't know how to express yourself. What you meant to say is that my mother is an unbearable tyrant and a bitch on wheels."

He shrugged again. She had to smile despite herself as she examined the wonderful width of those shoulders. She shook her head. "Mother seems to have taken an interest in the physical type," she offered suggestively.

"Must be in the family," he said.

She waited a moment and then burst out laughing. "So you've heard all about me!" She chuckled delightedly. "What have you heard?"

The back of his neck got red and the car sped up. Vicki laughed even louder, then stopped suddenly. "I asked you to drive slowly," she reminded him. "I'm in no rush to get home. Tell me about yourself. What makes Mother take such an interest in you? Or does she? Are you sleeping with her? When did she hire you, anyway?"

"Day before yesterday. And I'm not doing anything with her. I don't particularly like her."

"Tell me why you don't like her."

"Because she won't let me work in one of the factories. I have to drive a lousy—" He lifted his hands from the wheel in a mocking gesture. "You see, I—never mind."

Vicki frowned. She tried to look at his profile by leaning over and was momentarily surprised at the sincerity and vulnerability she saw.

"Hey, you really mean that? Are you crazy or something? Why would anybody want to work in a factory?"

"That's the size of it."

"Too bad."

"Why don't you talk to her?" he asked. "Tell her I'm so repulsive to you that you can't stand riding with me."

"What makes you think you're not?"

"I'm not that lucky. Why don't you tell your mother that you can't stand me around?"

"I will not. I don't stick my nose into Mother's affairs. No sir. I know very well which side my bread is buttered on. If she wants you to drive the car or to be the court jester or to dance ballet or to sleep with her—I don't give a shit."

He was quite disturbed, as she could tell from the fascinating tightening of the muscles of his neck and arms.

"Sorry, Big Boy," she said. Then suddenly: "Jesus, you're beautiful. Stop the goddamn car, will you? I want to get out."

He pulled to the side of the deserted road and stopped. She leaned over to grip his shoulder; hard as a rock it was.

"You might as well get used to it," she said evenly. "I just don't know how to keep my hands off a big, strong man like you."

Moving away from her, he slid out of the car and held open the rear door. She stepped out and put her hand on his forearm. There were convulsive movements in her throat.

"It makes me mad," she said, her lips quivering.

He did not ask what made her mad.

"You know why I'm mad? Because they all know me so well...so well. Why the hell did Mother send you? I'll tell you why. They all think I'm an alley cat who needs the biggest tomcat she can get. Well, they're right."

The pressure of her fingers on his arm increased.

"They're so right," she continued. "So right."

"Get back in the car," he said, trying to release her hold.

She allowed herself to be helped into the back seat, where she lay back, her hair sprawled over the rich cloth of her seat, her dress up, her white thighs waiting for him. She began to pull him down.

"No, ma'am!" he spat out, jerking back.

"Yes!" she lashed sibilantly. Her nails scraped along his jacket. Tears sprang to her eyes. "Yes! Yes!"

But he was away and had already slammed the door between them. He moved into the front seat quickly and the car was moving again.

She lay with her eyes closed tightly, her body writhing in a pain of wanting.

"Bastard," she moaned.

Later, when she sat up, she lit a cigarette with trembling hands. "Why didn't you want to lay me?" she asked hoarsely.

He shrugged. "Just tell your mother that I'd be better in one of her factories."

She kicked the back of his seat weakly and her eyes were wet again, for she knew with a flaring anger that the big man was playing her for a fool, teasing her. She cursed.

"Sure," he said, glancing at the overhead mirror. "But don't forget to tell your mother what I asked you."

"Oh, shut up!" she cried.

★★★

"What did you think of him?" asked Janet after she and her daughter were settled in the music room, cool drinks in hand.

"Who?"

"The chauffeur, of course. Didn't you notice him?"

Vicki raised her glass descriptively to indicate the stratosphere. "How could I help but notice him? I'm sure I've never seen such a—what the hell is he doing, wearing William's cap on that big head of his?"

"He's not really—we still have William. The point is, do you like him?"

"What difference does that make?"

"He's attractive, you must admit."

Vicki frowned prettily. "Sure. But he's an absolute prude."

"How would you know that?"

"Simple. I invited him to make love to me and all he said was—well, he refused. I'm certainly not going to tell you what he said."

"You *invited*?" In alarm, Janet sat forward. "My heavens, Vicki, you certainly haven't learned any restraint in the time you've been away."

"Oh come on, Mother." The girl's lips twisted humorously. "The first thing you ask me after not having seen me for a year is whether or not I find your chauffeur attractive. So I suspect you didn't intend that I restrain myself with him. What's so important about him, anyway?"

Her mother edged back uncomfortably in her seat. "Well, I just thought you could be more subtle."

"Why should I bother being subtle or anything else? What's in your very pretty head, Mother?"

"Don't try flattering me. It happens that I just realized this morning that you would probably find Morrison attractive. Don't be offended, please. And, well, I wanted to say that I had no particular objection if you... well...."

"And it just so happens," Vicki said thoughtfully, "that you hired him two days ago, on the same day you called me long distance to rush home. I had to leave a man with his pants still dangling around his ankles."

"Stop that kind of talk, Vicki!"

"Well, it looks mighty neat to me," Vicki insisted, "him here and you calling me home this way."

Her mother's face softened. "I've had business problems, and I want you and Lance to settle down here in

Greenville. I don't like living alone anymore. I want you to stop running around the country and with a lot of men. There are some nice young men around here you could marry who belong to good families."

"Is that where the chauffeur comes in? A lover to help my husband carry the load?"

"He's not the chauffeur, not really." Janet took a breath and started again. "All right, I can see you haven't changed. You still don't know how to conduct yourself or talk politely or even restrain yourself."

"He restrained. Your chauffeur did the restraining."

"Fortunately. What must he think of you! Vicki, I don't know what I'm going to do with you. But I do want you home with me. You and Lance. You must both think of settling down now that I'm getting older."

"Oh, Mother, cut that out, please. Just say what you have in mind. This beating about the bush..."

Janet brightened. "We'll have lots of parties and things, dear, these next few weeks. Tonight, Carlotta's mother will give you a welcome home party. You can meet all the eligible young men, too. These are the kinds of things where everyone is encouraged to invite relatives from out of town. You're liable to meet some nice men."

"Oh, then Morrison is for *you*, not for me."

"Now stop being silly. You sound just like Lance."

"Where is he, anyway? Drinking in the cottage?" She waved the thought away with an airy hand. "Go on, Mother."

"Well, if you decide to stay home—and I've decided that—you won't have to pick up all the factory hands if you want to have a fling now and then. Life gets too messy when you do that. I'm sure Morrison is a man who ought to be able to fill all your needs while you're looking for Mr. Right."

"Mother, I don't blame you for blushing."

Janet lowered her gaze. "A fact is a fact."

"It'll be a pleasure," Vicki said, smiling. "Why didn't you say all this in the first place?"

"It's a delicate subject, you'll have to admit."

"Not to me," said the daughter, shrugging her thin shoulders. Then, with spontaneity, she added, "And if I decide to get married and settle down, as you put it, do you promise I can keep Morrison on the side?"

"It'll probably be necessary," Janet said dryly.

"Tell me, Mother," Vicki asked suddenly, "how'd you happen to pick out Morrison?"

Janet leaned backward. She moistened her lips. She was tempted to tell Vicki about The Dream, Vicki in that man's arms, the man she had seen only for an instant's glimpse that evening coming out of Bart's office. But quickly, she decided against this revelation. For one thing, her daughter would laugh; she always laughed and scoffed. And somehow, she didn't know why, it would (in some subtle manner) give Vicki an upper hand in their relationship if she knew about The Dream, Janet sensed. Best not to mention it. Perhaps there was an element of guilt—ridiculously, Janet told herself—because—yes—she had been watching those beautiful lovers in her dream, watching in hiding, as though she should not have been watching. Silly; in her own dream! But looking back, there was something about it that made her uncomfortable. It was best to forget it entirely.

"Never mind, then," said Vicki, observing her mother's thoughtfulness with curiosity. "You picked a lulu of a man anyway. One thing, though. I don't think he likes to take orders from you."

The woman grunted. "Nobody likes to take orders from me. But he does."

"Who does that?" said Lance, strolling into the room, preceded by a sloshing highball glass. "You ladies have been conspiring, I can tell. In fact, I listened a bit, toward the end."

"Hi," said Vicki.

"Hello, Sis. How was New Orleans?"

"Hot."

"That's very sad."

Janet signaled Vicki that they would continue their discussion afterward, then patting Lance on the shoulder, she excused herself from the room. Lance held up his glass and squinted through it at his mother's retreated figure.

"So now, dear sister," he said jovially, "you know why you've been summoned back to the old homestead. I got the facts about your hired stud from Mother yesterday. I'm still drinking to drown out the taste of it."

"Sure, I'll bet that's the only reason you're drinking today." Vicki turned on him sharply. "Keep out of it, Lance. I don't need her muscle boy; I can get my own boyfriends. But if that's the way Big Mama wants to play it, who the hell cares? You back off. Be careful, baby, or Mother'll take your little bottle away."

He chuckled and fingered his collar as though he'd suddenly become warm. "You're right. That's the only threat that works. Dear Mom, who holds the great big bottle opener in her wee little hand and the key to all the saloons in the world...."

"Stop complaining. She's very good to both of us, and you know it. She never asks us to do anything we'd rather not do or be anything that we're not. Especially that. If she wants to see us settle down—well, that's not such an evil thing. Who's she got lined up for you?"

He shook his head uncaringly. His eyes had already misted, and he was apparently too choked up to speak. Vicki looked at him in alarm.

"Now don't start that crap. I don't want one of your Good Ol' Mother crying jags. Sorry I brought up the subject."

"But you were right," he managed to say. "She's been so good to us, and I don't appreciate her. Not half enough." He wiped a sleeve of his light corduroy jacket across his eyes.

"Yes, all you need is a slight reminder," Vicki said ironically. "Just keep remembering it and don't interfere with me. If she wants to have that gorgeous hunk of man around the house, it's okay with me. Maybe I'll even marry him and get some decent blood into the family."

"You wouldn't!"

"No, of course not. But don't you go discussing the matter with him, please."

Lance drained his glass with a gulp and started toward the door.

"Won't say a word to him," he said over his shoulder. "Won't even talk to him. Big men only remind me of how puny I am. So he's all yours, Sister."

Now some playback. We've been making a videotape recording of everything you've said and done and here it comes on television— watch the screen. You're seeing yourself the way the rest of us see you. There, see that musclebound stiffness, the way you hold yourself so straight and aloof. You communicate coldness, don't you see?

Do you know what some of the others call you? "The Great Stoneface"! Do you think it's unmanly to show how you feel? How are people going to know where you stand unless you express your feelings? If you don't tell them how you feel or send out cues or signals, then you defeat people who want to communicate...you frighten them away. After all, sexuality is only one facet of your personality. Do you think you become another person as soon as you lie down? So it should be clear that an attack on sex itself will get you nowhere. You've got to break out of the right personality you've constructed for yourself, find a new transcendence, new limits....

CHAPTER 6

C arl..."

"Vicki..."

The blonde girl bounded onto the tennis court despite Bill Draper's readiness to serve, his bronzed arm upheld. He dropped his racquet to his thigh and looked embarrassed and masculine as Vicki hugged her friend right there on the red dust of the court. Carlotta suddenly looked as though she were being gripped by a creature from outer space.

"I'm all sweaty," she objected with laughter.

"What the hell do I care?" Vicki pulled her along toward the clubhouse. "You take a shower. I'll wait. Where were you all morning? I thought you'd be waiting for me with Mother."

Carlotta's face clouded, but her friend went on blithely.

"Anyway, I'm glad to see you," Vicki said. "You're *glad to see me*, you little bitch? I missed you like hell, you know that?"

"Ditto."

"Did you really?"

The dark beauty nodded vigorously. Yes, she had missed her friend and she hadn't even realized it until perhaps this very moment. As a child, she had felt chained to Vicki, as well as physically and spiritually offended at the girl's earthiness, but she hardly noticed the objectionable side of Vicki now. The girl was part of her life, she thought as they entered the shower room; a part of her character, like it or not.

"You wait here," Carlotta said at her locker. "I'll be through in a jiffy."

"Nuts. I'll come in. I've seen you shower before."

She followed her friend into a room of stall showers and sat on a bench and watched Carlotta undress.

"Wow!" she intoned humorously.

Carlotta blushed. She felt ridiculous in her desire to cover her body as she walked timidly into the shower. Vicki vetoed her suggestion to draw the curtain, saying they wouldn't be able to talk that way, and in its stead, Carlotta turned the faucet on as hot as she could bear to make a screen of steam.

"You're built better than I am, you know that?" Vicki shouted after watching her friend soap herself. "Not even a dimple on your ass, no extra fat, a bust like a statue. Carl—"

"Mmm?"

"Anybody ever nibble on those things? Like a man?"

"VICK—"

"You mean you've never had a man? What the hell's the matter with you?"

Carlotta turned off the water and reached gratefully for her towel.

"Tell me," Vicki said inquisitively.

"Never mind that. Talk about something else."

"You sound like a schoolteacher. All right, get those fresh shorts on. There's a man outside I want you to meet. He'll change your mind about things."

"Who's that?"

"You'll see. Maybe after you do, you'll want to know what it's like."

As Carlotta might have guessed, it was the big man. He was seated on the porch in front of the club in the shade of the black sedan. He stood up as the girls neared the car.

"Mother's new chauffeur and general handyman. He goes by the name of Morrison," said Vicki, smiling up at him. She glanced at Carlotta. "Ever see such a hunk of a man?"

"I met Mr. Morrison yesterday," the dark girl admitted, reddening despite a resolve not to respond in any way. "I mean I saw him at the tea."

From the corner of her eye, she spotted Janet Harper seated in the back of the car. She nodded politely but the woman did not acknowledge her greeting. Vicki laughed.

"If you saw him yesterday, I'll bet you have the very idea I was trying to convince you about in the shower, eh, Carl? And without any prompting from me, either."

Carlotta shot her a warning glance. She did not dare to look toward the back of the sedan again.

"Don't worry," Vicki continued airily. "He doesn't understand. I've been trying all morning to get him to make love to me, and I don't think he knows what it means." She turned to Morrison. "Do you, handsome?"

He looked hard at Carlotta. She did not return his look.

"Making love means different things to different people," he said, his eyes remaining on the darker girl, to Vicki's annoyance.

"Let's take a ride," she ordered tersely. "Would you like to come, Carlotta?"

The girl shook her head. "No thanks. I'm going home and I have my car here. See you at my house tonight. Goodbye. Goodbye, Mrs. Harper."

The woman in the back seat did not answer.

Tonight. Tonight Carlotta's mother was to give a party to welcome Vicki home. Tonight the three people before her now would be with her again. Morrison would be there, she was sure. She wished that she could be ill, too ill to attend any social function at all for weeks. Especially the party at her own house tonight.

"Well, don't look so unhappy about it or I won't come," Vicki called brightly to her as the car moved off. Settling back in her seat, Vicki turned to her mother. "Carlotta's still beautiful as ever, isn't she?" She glanced toward the front. "Did you know, Mother, that our Mr. Morrison has a life's ambition? He has one great, big love. He told me."

Morrison's hands tightened around the steering wheel and his back hunched under his jacket. There was no answer from Janet, but he felt that she was watching him. A glance in the overhead mirror confirmed his suspicion.

"And what is our chauffeur's life ambition?" she asked impassively.

He cursed himself for having told even this little bit about himself to Vicki. There was nothing that made a man more vulnerable than the announcement of his ambitions. In the mirror, his eyes met Vicki's, but he gave her no message except disapproval. The car had swerved in the interval of their silent communication. He steered to the middle of the road again.

"Keep your eyes on your driving," Janet commanded.

Vicki came in breathlessly. "Mother, let me finish telling you about Morrison. Do you know what he wants to be? A maintenance man. Fixing machines in factories. He really wants it. It's like a passion."

The car glided silently as the older woman quietly absorbed this bit of information and tried to understand what was going on between the two others in the car.

"Morrison," she asked finally, "what experience have you had?"

He didn't want to say anything because he didn't trust her.

"Well?" she insisted.

"I worked at it in the East when I was a kid. Tended machines in a few small plants. Rag factory, shoe factory. I did maintenance, I was the assistant to the foreman. I'm a good machine man."

"I'm sure you are," she answered, bored with the idea.

The subject seemed to have been dropped when, a few minutes later, he observed Vicki through the mirror whispering in her mother's ear and Janet shaking her head. Then, finally, the woman shrugged and leaned forward. She instructed him to take the next road left. They came on the road to one of her bottling factories.

When he opened the door for her, she said tersely, "Come with me."

The factory was brightly illuminated with fluorescent lights that stretched from one end of the long single-story structure to the other. As the trio entered, the men who had been bending over machines or staring at bottles that passed before eerily lit magnifying glasses raised their heads and quickly returned to their tasks.

A tall man wearing a grease-stained apron, the foreman, came forth from the machinery to greet them. He was not in the least obsequious in the presence of his employer, and Morrison liked him on sight. Janet asked who the machine maintenance man was. It was a man named Joe.

"Send Joe to me," she told the foreman.

He left and returned with a short, dark man who wore an even greasier apron.

"Mrs. Harper," the man mumbled.

"Joe is the man who keeps all the machines here in running order," Janet elaborately explained to Vicki and

Morrison. "Joe, this is my daughter. And this is my chauffeur."

Joe let his gaze travel over them.

"My chauffeur," she went on, "wants your job, Joe."

Morrison froze. The maintenance man looked up at him in puzzlement and leaned forward instinctively. Morrison didn't move. Joe looked to Janet.

"That's what he told me," she said icily.

"No," said Vicki.

They all turned to her.

"It isn't true," Vicki said in a funny voice.

She turned to Morrison, but he was already on his way out. He could hear her running after him, but he didn't wait. At the car, he slid into the front seat. She went into the back and stared wordlessly ahead of her, waiting for her mother.

When Janet returned and sank down beside her daughter, she said clearly, loud enough for Morrison to hear every word, "I didn't understand any of that, Vicki. I wish you'd make up your mind. Morrison!" she called out to him. "I suppose my daughter wanted to teach you a lesson. If it was necessary to do so, then I approve. I hope you've learned your lesson. And I hope you'll forgive me, anyway."

Without an answer, he started the car. Not another word was said during the ride back to the Harper estate.

Let it happen to you. Let everything happen to you. Let anything happen to you. Let someone piss on you and degrade you utterly. You respect your precious self too much. You protect yourself too well. You're an armored man. The Zenrin says, "To save life, it must be destroyed. When utterly destroyed, one dwells for the first time in peace."

Go out and hit bottom. Get to a place where the modern scene, the relevant scene, the socialist scene, is no longer there to protect you. Get out of the cities, find a more basic America. Go on the road, let things happen to you, get locked up, get pissed on, hit bottom, hit bottom....

CHAPTER 7

Couples and singles, they walked in and out of groups made up of other couples and singles, drinks in hand, moving along and laughing (or swaying), pressed against their partners in semi-sexual contact, dancing, drinking, waiting, dancing, drinking again, the muted band playing. The men were sleek, young and competitive, though not as competitive as the women.

Morrison sat in an armchair, drinking more than most. In Carlotta Ford's home. He knew that if he should get out of the chair, he would tower; the scene would go suddenly out of kilter. There was a girl standing at the edge of a group, a somewhat more sober group than others, an older group, though she, herself, couldn't have been more than twenty. She was throwing curious glances his way. Her hair was dark, like a little cap on her head. Gorgeous. But she couldn't hold a candle to Carlotta. Class, but not the top of the class. Carlotta had that spot all picked out.

He got up from the chair. He wasn't drunk at all. It was ridiculous how much he could drink without feeling a damned thing. Alcohol became lost in the immensity of his body. Carlotta was standing alone by the dead fireplace when he found her. She caught his eye as he was coming, and he detected that hunted expression he noticed earlier in the day at the country club. He knew that she would try to frustrate his attempt to talk with her and to be alone with her.

He wondered, seeing the resignation, a tired resignation of her gray-green eyes, whether it would be conceited of him to think that all the symptoms of fright and flight she exhibited were the symptoms of a growing and reluctant interest in him. Could two people find each other so quickly? Could they both find precisely what they had been looking for all their lives? If she were falling for him, it would be the classic explanation of her avoidance, of the panic he had begun to sense in her. The kind of "cold" girl that Janet Harper had labeled her, the kind of person he wanted and needed most of all, might well react in this furtive fashion when it hit her.

If all this were true, then he must help her to see that they were right for each other. He would be patient, just as he would need her patience later. For now, he certainly did not want to frighten her away.

"Hello. You look tired," he said, standing before her, assured that she could not easily escape him without at least an exchange of words. "Too much tennis, perhaps?"

"Tired? No, I'm not tired, I don't believe."

"You're very beautiful," he said suddenly.

Panic was again in her face. "Have you seen Vicki? I need to find her," she blurted out.

"Why? You can very well see Vicki five or ten minutes from now. She'll still be here. I can see that I make you extremely nervous and you want to get rid of me. I think that either you're too conceited to imagine a man wanting to talk to you who isn't madly in love with you or...."

He could see now a laughter in her eyes.

"You don't usually talk in such long sentences, do you, Mr. Morrison?"

"I don't usually have to argue to make someone stand still."

"I'm the hostess. I have to circulate."

"Nuts."

She cooled visibly. "Then what is it you want?"

"What *I* want?" He felt unsure. "Well, I had hoped you would dance with me."

"Certainly," she answered. "Later, perhaps."

She made a polite little motion with her head and went past him. He did not turn but stared at the brick fireplace. He felt like a fool. Vicki was a bitch, and she would never reach him this way.

"Mr. Morrison! I believe you know who I am."

He turned and faced Carlotta's father. Sleek gray hair, smooth.

"Yes, of course, Mr. Ford."

"Can we talk honestly with each other?"

With a feeling of apprehension, Morrison nodded. Was the man going to ask about his interest in Carlotta?

Ridiculous. Snap out of it. Anyway, the man couldn't possibly know about his personal problem.

"I understand you came in with Ned Amsterdam," the older man was saying. "I wonder if you'll tell me where he hid the report."

Morrison frowned. "I don't know anything about any report. You knew Amsterdam? He did say he was coming here to see a friend. Was it you?"

"I assume he meant me, yes."

"Well, I assure you, Mr. Ford, I know nothing about—"

"Morrison, I understand why you're being so cagey. You've been told to be careful."

"That's not so, Mr. Ford."

"But we have a lot in common," the man went on. "That is, we have a person in common, my daughter. And this can ease the way in our relationship and your relationship. You see, my daughter is not really experienced with men."

"I know that. And I assure you, Mr. Ford—"

"No assurances necessary. I have nothing against you, young man. In fact, I'm looking forward to a fine friendship."

"You mean if I can give you the report."

Mr. Ford smiled. "Did he tell you what was in the report?"

"He never mentioned any report."

"Morrison, if you only realized how foolish all this lying is. It's all a private matter concerning me and Mr. Amsterdam. I could complain to the police, you know."

The big man frowned at him thoughtfully. "Are you serious? You'd be a prime suspect in a murder."

Carlotta's father had evidently thought of that but had wanted to see if mention of the police would frighten him.

"I'd advise you to forget about the report and just let sleeping dogs lie," Morrison said gently.

"You won't help me, then?"

"You just won't believe me, will you?"

"He had the report," Ford insisted. "He was bringing it here. He was supposed to bring it to me. Now it's gone."

"Yes, there seems to be a mystery. Now, if you'll excuse me, Mr. Ford."

The older man watched him go by with a burning silence.

Morrison found Vicki sitting on a young man's lap, her hand inside the blushing man's jacket, feeling his chest as though she were a man and as though he had breasts to fondle. Morrison jerked his head and she was off the young man's knee and at his side.

"I've been waiting for my master to summon me," she said wittily. "Get us some drinks, handsome."

He fetched the drinks and she gazed up at him attentively.

"Well, I'm here," she quipped. "I hope the party is softening you up for me because later, I'm going to rape you."

"I've been talking to your friend Carlotta," he said, knowing she must have seen him with the girl. "What gives? Why is she so scared of me? Did you or your mother put a gag over her mouth?"

"What are you talking about?" Vicki gulped her drink with annoyance.

"Is she always this way? The first day I saw her, I thought we hit it off kind of good. I mean friendly-like. Now she seems to hate my guts."

"Does that bother you so much? You're not willing to let it go at that, are you? You're a brave man, Morrison."

"Sure. You're going to tell me now what a cold dish she is."

Vicki laughed. "She can give a man a terrible runaround. She's not like me—warm-blooded, I mean. Candid, I mean. Oh no, she's cold and secretive. She's like an iceberg and as far away as the nearest one. Mother used to send her along on double dates with me. Did you know that?"

He shrugged. "I don't know much of anything about any of you. I'm a stranger here, remember?"

"Mother sent her with me so she could freeze down the boys I heated up. Do you know what I mean?"

He showed on his face that he knew what she meant.

"She just never learned to put out. It's sad. There are women like that, you know. Not only with boys; with girls also. I was just about her only real friend when we were growing up. Except maybe Nelly, who was just a hanger-on. I was practically her only friend, and we weren't really close. She was always disapproving of me."

"She disapproves of me, too, I think."

Vicki stared up at him thoughtfully, her eyes flashing. "I guess she froze you so hard that you haven't gotten over it, huh? Stay with me awhile and thaw out."

This he found he could do with no difficulty because she was affable and she was fun. They shifted in and out of groups, and the groups were always sorry to see them go on to the next one.

"Having fun?" Janet Harper asked. She addressed them, he thought fleetingly, as she would a married couple, waiting, as it were, for a representative answer from one or the other.

"Marvelous!" Vicki beamed. "I'm thawing Morrison out."

"Good. He needs it."

But the mother's glance said not too much thawing out at once. A not-so-young man asked Vicki to dance. She said, "Wait around for me, Morrison."

He didn't wait. He scanned the room, finding Carlotta, resolution bursting inside him. Striding to her once again, his face was hard and grim.

"I'm glad I found you alone again," he said unsmilingly, almost argumentatively.

She looked up sharply. "I'm not alone. He'll be back in a moment with some drinks."

"Who?"

"Someone. A man. Are we going to argue, Mr. Morrison?"

He blew out his breath. "All right. No argument. It's just that the other day I had a feeling about us, that we could talk to each other. I still feel that way. There's no one in this town I'd rather get to know. I mean that sincerely."

She searched his face for a moment.

"But there are others," she said softly, "who desire your attention and your presence more than I do, aren't there?"

He grinned. "All the girls are panting, yes. But I can't right now. Right now, I'm busy with you. Can't I attend to them later?"

"I don't think that would be wise."

"Don't sound so mysterious."

"I really think you're wanted elsewhere," she insisted.

She tilted her head an inch to the left. He followed her gaze. Vicki, he saw, had ditched her dance partner and was standing, glass in hand, staring at them. Perhaps she had meant to test him this way.

When he looked down at Carlotta again, she was attempting to slip away. He thought of holding her arm, forcing her to dance with him, but he didn't dare. Deserted, he made his way back to the blonde girl. Her blue eyes were shining and laughing. He stood in front of her awkwardly, as if he'd been sent on an errand, stiff like a kid told by one adult to report to another. Which was how he felt.

She seemed to know how he felt, too. And she wasn't angry. She lifted her white arms and put them around his neck and pressed against him, swaying in time with the music, spilling some of the drink in her hand down his neck.

He stood that way for a second, feeling her breasts burning into his body, thinking that he could define the very outlines of her nipples. In what he hoped was an easy and inoffensive gesture, he released her and salvaged the tipped glass from her hand. His heart was pounding loudly, much to his own disgust.

So that he wouldn't hurt her feelings, so he would not let her know there was any wrong emotion between them, he sipped from her drink, from the very spot where her lipstick had stained the glass, before handing it back to her.

"That means you love me," she said. She was smiling and her face was pure and wholesome. "I've been waiting for you with great feeling the last few minutes while you were busy elsewhere. I thought you should know that."

"You're a nice girl to have waiting for me," he offered, meaning it in a way, his face expressionless because he knew they were now being watched by all kinds of people after that hug, not wanting her pawing him again. He could never know what a willful girl like Vicki would do next. From this mood she was liable to go right into some kind of screaming sex scene. But she seemed stable for the moment.

"Two beautiful men came over since I ditched that guy to wait around for you," she said, lifting her head imperceptibly in a challenge. "I sent them away, waiting for you. Seems I've been waiting for you."

"I'm flattered."

"No you're not, you bastard."

"No scene, Vicki, I'm warning you. I'll walk right out on you."

"Boy, are you touchy. I wasn't going to—"

"Just don't."

"But honey, don't you like the idea that I turn away every man except you?"

"Maybe you shouldn't. Maybe they're sensitive."

Vicki giggled. "They're not. Not with someone as rich as a Harper. You—you're the only one who has to be handled with kid gloves." She brought her body close to him again but kept her arms to herself. "I think you like me better than you admit, don't you?"

"Sure. You're a lot of fun. You were sweetness itself a little earlier today in the factory."

Her teeth showed. "I don't like being teased about that. I'll forget it if you'll do likewise." Her eyes looked dead for a moment. "Morrison—"

"I know. You want to apologize."

"Yes."

"For being the complete bitch."

She didn't look at him.

He repeated, "For being the complete bitch."

"All right. I apologize. I really do."

"It hurt. You know why, Vicki?"

"I think I know."

"Because you reminded me that...no, never mind."

"You trusted me," Vicki said.

"Don't even think that. I was just stupid. An old habit of us people, being stupid."

"No difference. Please listen, you beautiful man. I want to make it up to you."

"Why is that?"

"I don't like being able to push people around, that's all. I don't. That's the truth. Sure, you got me mad, but nobody likes an uneven fight. And anyway, I never laugh at the idea of work. There's at least something real and dignified about hard work. I never laugh at that."

"All right, how're you going to make it up to me?"

"Nights—"

"That again! I thought—"

"Nights," she said again with emphasis. "I can get you into the factory for a while. A watchman at one of the places is an old pal of mine. He used to like me as a toddler and all that sort of stuff."

"I'm not sure I understand this."

"Yes you do, silly. I saw the way you looked at those machines this afternoon."

"What did you see?"

"Never mind what I saw, but it all showed on your face. If you want to work on the machines, then I can get you in some nights. Maybe tomorrow."

He went into silence and then, a moment later, asked in a level voice, "But what's the point?"

"So I can make it up to you. It was rotten of me. I know I violated your trust in me. Anyway, I like to watch a man doing work he likes to do."

"You want to watch," he said dryly.

"Well, I have to be with you so your evenings will be accounted for, don't I?"

"Why do we have to account for my evenings?"

Vicki looked at him as though he were stupid. "Mother would never let you do this if she knew. So we let her think you're chauffeuring me around or even that we've been having a ball somewhere."

"Why wouldn't she want to let me work in the factory? Why is it so important to her?"

Her eyes held his briefly and she tilted her head. "Well, think of it this way. If Mother wants you under her thumb, the one thing she doesn't want you to have is any kind of dignity or private satisfaction. She mustn't know, that's all." Vicki waited for his answer to show on his features. "It's yes, isn't it?"

"Okay," he said. "How about later tonight?"

"Possibly. If we can. After you bring Mother home. Now do you believe I'm your friend?" She moved closer. "Take a walk with me now. You'll swear you never had a better friend."

He chuckled softly.

"Come on," she urged. "I'll let you take complete charge. You can make all the moves."

"You mean you'll let me make the conquest?"

"Please."

"Listen, Vicki—"

"Please, Morrison." She had him gripped around the waist.

"Vicki, I tried to tell you when I first met you that I'm not looking for that kind of relationship."

"You're making a fool of me," she said, drawing back.

"That's not true."

Her face tightened with controlled agony. "Everyone makes fun of a girl like me. They think it's a big joke just because I have to have it. They toy with me."

"I'm not toying with you," he said simply.

"Then why won't you sleep with me?"

He shrugged helplessly under her demanding, tearful stare. He thought of saying something light but couldn't bring it off.

"See, you can't even find a good excuse," she breathed. "But I'm your friend." Suddenly she was happy again. "I'm not going to put you on the spot. I can wait."

"That's kind of you."

"Oh, I know you want me all right," she went on. "I can see it in the pulse of your gorgeous neck when I look at you. But I'm not sure why you...maybe you're trying to teach me a lesson. Maybe you think that if I don't get it, I'll be cured. Is that just a crazy idea I've got about you? Well, nobody can teach me anything. You're not trying to cure me, are you?"

"I'm not trying to cure you, Vicki, believe me."

"If you want to cure me, all you have to do is sleep with me."

He didn't answer.

"I don't need a million men," she said. "Really just one good one."

He looked down at his hands.

"Say something, Morrison."

He didn't.

From across the room, Carlotta watched them. Everyone else did the same. After her first encounter with Morrison, Carlotta had no trouble avoiding him for the remaining hours of the evening. It was not even necessary to involve herself, as she did—hostess-like—with groups of people, with one smiling man after another. He remained with Vicki, dancing, drinking, her holding him disgracefully close at times, causing talk. There was no time for him to bother with another girl.

"We're rather well-off, aren't we, Dad?" Carlotta asked suddenly, turning to her parents. "I mean, we're fortunate, aren't we?"

He boomed out laughter. "Sure enough!"

Her mother smiled.

"Could you be happy if you didn't...if you weren't so well off?" Carlotta persisted.

He thought for a moment and chuckled. He shook his head with sheepish honesty.

"It wouldn't be easy. But I'd have you and your mother. That would be enough if times ever got rough. Hey, what kind of question is that anyway? Got anything catastrophic in mind?"

"Just hypothetical," she said, noticing that her mother was frowning.

Carlotta made her exit as soon as she could and went to her room, where she closed the door quickly behind her.

As she undressed, the scenes of the party passed unbidden before her vision. She recalled every movement Morrison made. She wondered if he knew what happened between Janet Harper and herself, the warning. No, she was sure he didn't quite understand the position she was in.

When she slipped into bed, she felt numb. Everything was strange. Her room. Her parents. Even herself.

An hour later, still staring at the dark ceiling, she thought not of him but of Vicki and Janet. She wondered if she knew them; if they were not strangers also. How utterly unreal that a man can become so important in the life of women that Vicki's mother would fight, as only a lioness would fight for her young, to shield him against other women.

How wonderful it would be, she mused, if all this intensity of feeling were happening not to Vicki, not to Janet Harper, but to Carlotta Ford.

No, you fool, she cried to herself. Didn't you see the concern on Mother's face? Didn't you hear the fear in Dad's booming laughter?

You have to see yourself as a nonrational being in the experiential-existential context, not as an intelligent or thinking man. Thinking will never cure you; you've got to be and find out what makes you be. And don't call this a form of therapy; call it behavioral modification. Learn new ways of thinking and behaving. Unlearn the dangerous ideas that are gripping you. A human has to actualize himself, become what he is meant to be. Bridge the difference between yourself and strangeness. Urinate. Yes, pull out your dick and urinate in front of all of us. Here, into the flowerpot. Open your fly....

CHAPTER 8

A ll right, it's around here," she said. When he stopped the car, he jumped out to go to the other side and hold open the door for her. Vicki called out into the dark gloom.

"Mr. Fulton?"

Footsteps approached the gate. "That you, Miss Harper?" His searchlight found them.

"Put down the light," she ordered, "before you blind us." The elderly watchman dropped the beam to the gravel and Vicki and Morrison followed him noisily down the path into the factory. "Did you cover the windows?" she asked him as he reached for the light switch.

The watchman answered in the affirmative. Soon one corner of the factory was blazingly alight and three pairs of eyes were blinking.

"I'll go now, Miss Harper," the old man mumbled self-consciously. "I'll just go up to my shed near the gate and come back here in an hour. That all right, Miss Harper?"

"Yes," she said stiffly. She glanced at Morrison.

"Just a minute, Mr. Fulton," he said. "Are there any machines out of order in this plant?"

"Machines? Out of order?" The watchman looked from him to Vicki again.

"Yes. Didn't Miss Harper explain that I was to work on the machines tonight?"

"Well..." He shrugged. "She mentioned it, but...."

The big man's eyes were intense. "But you figured we came here for some other reason."

The watchman backed away under Morrison's stare. Vicki moved forward suddenly.

"Will you show us the machines that need fixing?" she asked.

The old man pointed out one machine. "Out of commission for almost a week, that one."

"Why doesn't maintenance fix it?" Morrison asked.

Mr. Fulton shook his head. "He hasn't been able to yet, I guess."

"All right, I'll work on this one tonight."

"You mean you'll fix it, um, tonight? In an hour?"

"I'll try."

The watchman started to leave but turned back again. "To be honest, young fellow, I didn't think you'd tinker with the machines. No offense. Sam'll know something's wrong if you fix it, though, or even if the bolts and things are moved around. Know what I mean?"

"Then I'll leave it just as I found it," Morrison promised. "After I fix it, I'll put it out of order again."

Mr. Fulton shuffled out of the factory and the big man turned toward the ailing machine. He rested a palm familiarly against the metal. His eyes swept around the room and located a master switch and he strode over to it and threw it into the ON position. A faint hum greeted him, and the long belt began to move the length of the factory. He removed his jacket. He seemed to have forgotten Vicki entirely.

"Take off your shirt, too," said Vicki behind him.

"What'd you say?"

"Your shirt. You can't afford to get it dirty...greasy. It'll give us away."

He stripped off his shirt and undershirt and she took them from him. "Wear this," she said, handing him an apron she'd removed from a hook on the wall.

He turned to the machine and began to work. Soon, his hands were black with grease and there were unaccountable grease marks on his chest and shoulders. As Vicki watched, fascinated by the strain and play of his muscles, his body seemed to shine as though it were being invisibly oiled.

At the end of an hour, the watchman returned. Vicki raised a finger to her lips to silence him, and he joined her in watching the broad back wrestle with the machine. After a while, Morrison snapped a switch and stepped back. A piston rose slowly and fell, again and again, and the machine began to purr rhythmically. He turned and smiled, his teeth startingly white against his streaked face. Vicki and Mr. Fulton returned his smile.

"Now you've got to break it again," the old man said, not without humor.

Morrison nodded. "I'll mess it up easy-like. Sam'll have a simple time fixing it tomorrow."

The watchman chuckled. "Come on, I'll show you where to get washed up. Miss Harper, you make sure he don't leave no clues. And put that there apron back on the hook. Tomorrow, I'll have a private apron here for your gentleman friend. That is, if you'll be here tomorrow."

"If not tomorrow, then the following night," Vicki said brightly. "Hurry up, beautiful, and bust that machine again."

Outside, she slid into the seat beside him and smiled as he urged the car over the gravel. Soon they were on the dirt road.

"Hit the highway for Jefferson," she told him. "It's too early to go home, isn't it?"

He nodded, still excited by his labor, barely aware that she was beside him. But when they reached the highway, she turned on him.

She was like a crazed animal, holding onto his right arm, pressing it against her body, while he held the wheel with his left. He drove slowly, nearing Jefferson, wondering when they could break this deadlock and turn back. He didn't feel safe outside of Greenville, somehow. Maybe he was getting to feel like one of the family already, and the idea irritated him. He tried twice as hard to get his arm away from the ferocious girl.

"How the hell can I drive," he snapped, "with you tearing one of my arms off?"

"Bah, you old sourpuss. You're only doing forty-five." Vicki climbed up further on his arm. Against his biceps, he could feel her soft breast and the fluttering of the heart within. She held him with tenacious strength, his fist now straddled between her thighs. "Isn't this better than having it on the wheel?" she purred.

"Yeah, but it's not safe."

She tightened her thighs. His blood started boiling in his veins. She worked her leg against his. It took him a moment to realize she had shoved her foot on top of his and was pressing down on the gas.

"Faster!" she cried, rubbing her body against him as the car shot ahead wildly. "Faster—faster!" Then she began to scream and clutch at his clothes.

Above all, he had to concentrate on keeping the scene of the crime on the road with one hand, trying to get her foot off the gas at the same time. There wasn't any way to protect himself. She had him in a stranglehold that made it impossible to budge her and live at the same time.

He was not surprised to hear in the midst of this madness of breasts, legs, arms and screams the angry insistence of a police siren. He had been moving at least ninety an hour.

Headlights cut glaringly across his rearview mirror. Vicki loosened her grip; he jerked his arm and sent her flying to the end of the seat.

"You did it, kid," he told her, pulling the car sharply to the shoulder of the road. "Now get us out of it."

The police car had zoomed ahead and swerved around alertly, making a wide, menacing arc with headlights on the overhanging trees. Vicki lay back sulkily in her corner of the seat, and Morrison felt a tightening in his chest as the police car stopped. Well, what was there to worry about? The Harpers could certainly afford the price of a speeding ticket.

Did a Harper ever get a speeding ticket?

He glanced quickly at the blonde girl beside him. No, of course she didn't get tickets. They wouldn't dare. He felt better about it. As if to show his confidence in their situation, he reached a conspiratorial hand toward Vicki and touched her fingers lightly. Wordlessly, she jerked her hand away.

One of the cops, one with a wide, meaty face and his cap tilted back revealing short, wiry black hair, put his big hands on the window on Vicki's side. The other cop stood behind him.

"Your license," he growled briefly, staring across to Morrison.

"I don't have it with me, but I'm Janet Harper's chauffeur," he answered, looking over at Vicki. "This here is Mrs. Harper's daughter."

"Janet Harper's daughter?" The cop examined Vicki.

"Yes," said Morrison.

"You haven't got your license?"

"Not with me," Morrison repeated calmly. "But Mrs. Harper'll explain about that to you if—"

The cop opened the door on Vicki's side and looked at her full-bodied. "You Mrs. Harper's daughter?" he asked again, this time carefully.

"No," answered Vicki.

Morrison glared at her. The cop frowned and shot a look at his partner.

"Get out," he ordered. "This door." He motioned beckoningly to Morrison and stepped back a prudent distance.

Morrison slid out after Vicki, who stood like a truant schoolgirl, her face pinched. When Morrison got his feet on the ground, the cop opened his eyes in astonishment and anxiety at his size and reached a hand to his holster.

"No reason for that," Vicki said.

"No?" the other cop drawled. He was thinner than his partner. "Why not?"

Vicki's lips quirked. "He wouldn't hurt a fly, don't worry. Take his keys out," she told the thin cop, looking into the pig face of the other one. Skinny looked at Pig-face for confirmation and got a nod. He went around and took the keys out from the ignition.

"Now give them to me." Vicki held out her hand. "So he'll wait for me."

Pig-face became restless. "And where the hell are you going?"

"With you, handsome." Vicki took his arm. "You and your friend. We can settle this between us, can't we, like civilized people?"

"How's that?" But the cop didn't shake her off, his face revealing he knew what she meant. His voice became business-like. "How about your boyfriend?"

"I told you. He wouldn't hurt a fly."

Both cops looked him over for a moment.

"Let's go," Pig-face said finally.

The three of them went into the woods.

Morrison lit a cigarette and sat on the fender. At first, he tried to close his ears to Vicki's moans drifting toward him on the night wind and the murmurs of the cops, embarrassed, trying to shush her. But then he shrugged and blew out his breath and said to himself, "What the hell!"

The nature lovers eventually returned. A motley crew, he thought. The cops ambled lazily to their car without looking at him once. He couldn't help smiling at the way they acted. They must have figured out that the girl had used them the same way she would have used a tree and that they just happened to come along. Vicki came out of the woods slowly.

"Your dress is wrinkled," he said, grinning as he held the door open for her. "If your mother sees it, she's liable to think you made a man of me."

She pinched his cheek and slipped into the front seat. "Impossible," she mumbled.

He took the keys from her dress pocket and warmed the motor until the cops moved off. He lit two cigarettes and offered one to her. She held his hand and lightly kissed the ends of his fingers. Then she took the cigarette.

Starting the car, he said, "You can rest on me if you want."

She pivoted her rump and then her head was on his lap. There, she dragged deeply and slowly on her cigarette and blew smoke up at his face.

"You're all right now, aren't you?" he said, rumpling her hair.

"Fine," she said.

Then she handed him the cigarette and fell asleep after crying for a bit.

Let's try role-playing. You're my husband. You're annoyed at me. No...you're angry at me. You'd like to beat me. You want to twist my arm and get me to my knees. Twist it—yes, I mean it.

I wish I could reach you. Why did you come to a woman therapist after all this time? Did you really think something would come of it, something new? It was a mistake choosing me. The way you've rejected the image of your mother, a woman therapist is the last person you should....

Let's see if I can stir you. Pretend I'm your mother. It's your mother you want. Her lips are seeking out your private parts....

CHAPTER 9

Please sit down, Lieutenant," Janet said, glancing at her watch. "Gosh, it's after three. I've been out shopping. Hope I haven't kept you waiting here long?"

She didn't wait for his answer.

"Well, have you found your murderer?"

"As you know, we haven't," he said blandly. "But we can figure out the motive easily enough."

"Oh, really? What is that?"

"Power, Mrs. Harper."

"And how do you know that?"

He shrugged self-effacingly. "We are very clever and we have our ways."

"Yes, you big policemen certainly have your ways. And one of the ways I don't appreciate is your tendency to patronize me."

"I'm not patronizing you, Janet."

She seated herself across from him in the library and wagged her finger at him. "I think you often do. As a matter of fact, I've wanted for some time to take it up with you. It seems to me that you tend to flaunt your maleness. You evidently are of the opinion that your maleness gives you the right to behave like a male."

"That went over my head," he said with a chuckle. "How else—"

"I mean, Lieutenant, that I want you to stop acting like a male in my presence, with the intent, that is, of reminding me of my femaleness. It's presumptuous of you. And I consider it patronizing." She rose suddenly and said, tilting her head, "So far, you've managed to be reasonably subtle in reminding me that you're the male and I'm the female. Please keep it that way: subtle. Don't become crass and direct. That would really be offensive."

He attempted to laugh it off. "Janet, Janet...I think you've completely misconstrued—"

"No, I haven't. You have occasionally hinted, I believe, that a widow like myself could indeed use the ministrations of a good man like yourself. Please don't ever hint at that too broadly, Mr. Schwartz, or I might really feel put upon. Please remember at all times that you are nothing more than a—" She stopped. "No, I'll restrain myself. I'll try to be diplomatic. You tell me, Lieutenant, is it necessary for me to put you in your place?"

He stared at her through bulging eyes, his face a deep red. "No, not necessary." He chuckled again, but his eyes fell into narrow slits. "Janet, I refuse to be provoked. You sure have the darndest ways of deflating a man."

"Yes, I have. What was it you came here to tell me, Lieutenant?"

She could see his fists tighten inside his coat pockets.

"Nothing really much," he said genially. "Just want to keep you up to date on the investigation. But obviously now isn't the right time. Good day, Mrs. Harper."

When he'd gone, she summoned the maid, Diane. Janet was tired from a day at the dressmaker, but the maid had requested to speak with her earlier and it had somehow seemed urgent. When Diane entered the library, Janet said directly, "Now what is it you want to talk to me about?"

The younger woman hesitated. It wasn't like her to be tongue-tied. Janet felt as if she would explode. "Is there anything wrong, Diane? You look as though you're holding back the tides of doom."

"I don't know if you'd call it *wrong*, Mrs. Harper.... Well, yes, I suppose you would." The maid gestured as if to return to her cleaning duties, but her mistress's fingers tapping on the edge of the chair fastened her attention.

"Does it concern something you've done?" asked Janet. This was incredible. Was this bright girl becoming stupid or something? Or was she merely being coy?

"Nothing wrong," Diane insisted, as if she couldn't possibly be connected with something wrong. "But I do feel I have to tell you, even though I promised."

Janet began to feel uneasy. However, she refused to ask again. She just stared and waited. She could have kicked this girl for being so low.

Finally the maid blurted out, "Your son—well, I have to admit I had something to do with it. I was...ambitious."

"Yes, I'm sure of that. So what has that got to do with my son?" But suddenly, the older woman understood. "You can't possibly mean you've got ambitions about Lance?"

"I haven't forgotten that I'm a housemaid, Mrs. Harper. I'm simply stating that I'd be the perfect wife, especially from your point of view. I'm fond of Lance, but I would never demand all his devotion."

Janet stiffened, alert to danger. "Have you seduced my son?"

"No, I haven't." Diane smiled ironically. "That's exactly the point. I would never do that unless I asked you first."

The mistress was stunned by this extraordinary candor. For a moment, she was speechless. But Diane suffered no such loss of expression.

"It's not to say that no one has seduced Lance," she went on hurriedly. "Nelly has."

Janet looked at her blankly.

"It's true, Mrs. Harper. And I admit I was with her when she met him outside the bar. I should have tried to stop her...."

"Why didn't you?"

"I'm not sure. She's so desperately in love with him. But now I realize how wrong she'd be for him in every way. What a danger she really is."

"*Danger*? She's a catastrophe!!"

"I see that now. And I wish Carlotta had used better judgment. I wish she'd never encouraged Nelly to do what she did."

Janet paled at the mention of the beautiful Carlotta. Her rage swirled around the two of them: Carlotta and Nelly. It was now in words. Never had she felt threatened that any woman would take away her son, but suddenly Nelly seemed to be that threat. The anger flooding Janet made her almost faint.

She had been betrayed. They'd whispered together, all of them, and betrayed her. They'd pretended to jump at her every command but had secretly conspired to subvert her. They were clearly laughing at her.

"How dare you!"

Diane refused to meet her employer's eyes. She remained looking down. "You're right to be angry with me. I figured if Carlotta approved—"

"What did Carlotta have to do with it?"

"I only know what Nelly told me."

"Which is what?" Janet demanded harshly.

"She said Carlotta told her that if she loved someone, she'd...you know, the same way Carlotta intended to get Morrison."

"Are you sure, Diane? That she advised Nelly to—seduce my son?"

"I'm to blame also, Mrs. Harper."

"No, no, it's not your fault. You were influenced by her. She should have known better. She's had the benefit of upbringing." She looked at her maid as though for the first time. "I don't mean to imply that you don't know any better, but it is true that you never had the benefit of that kind of upbringing, and you haven't betrayed someone who brought you up since you were a child."

"I understand, Mrs. Harper. I'm grateful you don't blame me. I only wish...."

She said more, but Janet no longer heard her. Nelly and Carlotta, she thought bitterly. They'd done this to her deliberately. All along, she believed she controlled them, but they had whispered and snickered behind her back, plotting to take away the two men. They probably roared with laughter when they spoke of it.

Did they expect that she was going to stand still and watch it happen? Did they imagine that she was too old to fight?

"I want them all here in an hour," Janet said sharply. "Every one of them: Nelly, Carlotta and Morrison. I want you to call the girls, Diane, and tell them I'm expecting them. I don't care where they are or what they're doing. Have them here."

★★★

They sat in the library. Vicki was there, too. She listened to the accusations against Nelly, then spoke up.

"Well, why not?" she asked. "Lance is a man, surprising as it is to me, and men and women are apt to —"

"Shut up!" Janet's face flushed crimson. She turned to Nelly, her tone patient but strained. "And what did you expect? Did you think you were in the Middle Ages, Nelly? Do you expect me to force my son to marry you?"

The ugly girl opened her mouth to speak. Then she closed it and looked to Carlotta for help. Carlotta looked back blankly and thought: *The fool*. She turned her eyes away and glanced at Morrison, who was gazing rather sympathetically at Nelly.

"When a girl nowadays allows herself to be seduced or seduces a man," Janet continued, "she can't come running home the next day and ask to have her honor saved. You wanted to marry him, didn't you? You thought my son was such a weakling that—"

"That's not true!" cried Nelly.

"Did Carlotta tell you to do it?"

"Not really. She only said it would be all right if I did."

The silence that followed, the first mass intake of breath, was like a cloud in the room. Carlotta felt her body drain of life, a kind of paralysis. If a match were put to her numb feet, she was sure she would feel nothing. She could not avoid the burning gaze of Janet Harper, who suddenly returned to address Nelly.

"Carlotta said it was all right to do it—did she influence you to do what you did?"

Nelly lowered her eyes, offering no denial. The woman leaned back in her chair and looked around the group, skipping over her daughter, Carlotta and the unhappy Nelly. Her look fastened on Morrison. It was several seconds before she tore her attention from him and turned to Carlotta.

"May I ask, Carlotta, why you did this?"

The dark-haired girl remained silent. *The bitch*, Janet thought.

"Well?" Janet insisted. Then she added, "It is difficult for me to understand this."

Carlotta nodded coolly. She thought she knew the direction Janet was headed. But she was afraid to speak lest her voice quiver. Even now, the thought of such an exhibition of her fear would be a disgrace.

"I don't understand," Janet repeated, "because I always thought, Carlotta, that it was *you* who wanted to marry Lance."

Morrison's body stilled visibly. Nelly turned sharply to look at the other girl. Janet smiled at the effect her revelation had on the group. Vicki, glancing from one face to the next, wore a puzzled frown.

She doesn't understand what's happening, Carlotta thought grimly. Poor, naïve, sophisticated Vicki...she never really understood her mother's mind.

"Why is everybody surprised? I thought you all knew about Carlotta and my son," Janet said with apparent astonishment. "Perhaps I should have mentioned it formally, but she told me about her feelings only recently. Isn't that so, Carl?"

The girl declined to answer.

Nelly turned on her friend. "It's not true, is it? You couldn't."

When Carlotta didn't answer, Nelly said, "And yet you told me—you told me to—"

Carlotta's eyes blazed to shut the girl up. *You and your stupid Lance,* she thought. Look at what you're doing to *me,* not to you or to him; to *me.* And Morrison...he knew, she hoped, that of course she couldn't love that weakling. He must know that she was receiving an order. Or perhaps he believed that the order was a longstanding one and that she had chosen the cheap way out by sending Nelly to lure the weakling into marriage. That was probably what Morrison was thinking now—what a coward she was. That was what Janet wanted him to think, for she also understood that honor was not unimportant to Morrison. And how right they were; she was indeed a coward.

Janet pulled a cord for the maid to come. "Send in my son, please," she said when Diane arrived.

Lance came in looking pale, his step hesitant, as though he were a child entering the principal's office. He nodded vaguely at everybody and stood beside his mother's chair.

"Yes, Mother?"

"Sit down," she told him.

"I'll stand. What is it?"

"Nelly said you slept with her a few nights ago."

Lance, stunned, sank into a chair. He stared hypnotically around the room at the faces watching him. He couldn't look at Nelly.

"WHAT did you say?"

Janet repeated it in the form of an accusation.

"How can you say such a thing, Mother?" he cried.

"Lance—" Nelly began.

Janet cut her off. "You were drunk, weren't you, Lance?"

He shrugged helplessly.

"And you weren't exactly capable of defending yourself, were you?"

"Defending myself?" The idea struck him as outrageous. "I didn't sleep with anybody."

His mother sketched in briefly where the incident supposedly took place. Carlotta listened with half an ear, seeing the room through a fog, conscious of only one presence now. Morrison's.

Now, she thought—as though the sun had pierced the fog surrounding her—I can still save myself. I can still have his respect if I do the one thing he's waiting for me to do. He must be waiting...or else why would he be so interested in this horrid scene involving a stupid girl who'd given herself away for nothing to a drunken weakling who either couldn't or wouldn't remember the gift? Yes, he's waiting for me to say right now, say aloud, that under no condition would I marry Lance Harper or anyone else, no matter what the threat was.

Why not? she asked herself. What have I got to lose? Janet will have to punish me and my parents anyway for what I've already done. The worst will happen. So why not take Morrison—tell Janet to her face that I'm going to take him whether Janet likes it or not.

But hadn't Janet foreseen this? Of course she had. And she was not going to do anything to Carlotta and her parents, not now. She was going to let everything stay as it was. That would be the worst punishment: leaving Carlotta in the same emotional storm and with the same conflicts as before, only now there was the threat of Lance and a sense of loss over a stranger who had come to town only a few days ago.

She looked up suddenly and saw that he had been watching her all along. Yes, he was waiting. Janet was also regarding her. Even Vicki was staring, seemingly at a loss for words. There was a dreadful silence. Everyone seemed to be waiting for her.

Carlotta's brain began to swim. No, she couldn't make any decisions now. She put her head in her hands and began to sob.

There was no stopping the strange, strangled sounds issuing from her lips. They burst forth like water behind a broken dam.

She heard Morrison rise and walk from the room. Then she heard the others leave. She was alone, she thought, until a hand fell on her shoulder. Quickly she looked up, praying with trembling lips that it was Morrison who had returned, that he would somehow take charge of the whole mess and straighten it out. But it was only Nelly, her wet eyes gazing down.

"I'm so sorry," Nelly offered. "But I can see now that—that it was a noble thing for you to have done."

"What?" Carlotta said uncomprehendingly.

"Loving Lance and yet wanting me to have a chance. You're so beautiful and I'm...well, it was so utterly decent of you. But I want you to realize that it'll make no difference between you and Lance. He doesn't even remember that night."

Carlotta punched her hands together. "Oh, get out of here!" she cried. "Leave me alone!"

★★★

Much later, the house was silent. In the room behind the big bay windows of the right wing it was dark, still too early for the ghostly light of dawn.

In the darkness, Janet Harper slept alone in the large bed. Suddenly, she sat up, her heart rocketing inside her chest, her eyes wide with a look of fear, her hands flailing the emptiness of black air. She was wet with perspiration beneath her lovely night attire.

She stared at the window and around the wide room as though she expected to see a stranger in her bedroom. Then, puzzled, so that her face looked even older than that of a woman only in her forties, she craned to look at the luminous clock on the table beside her bed. It was twenty-five minutes after four.

The exact time made no difference, of course; it was too early, that was all. And at first, she did not know why she had awakened.

And then she knew.

It had been The Dream.

The same Dream.

There was the man. She knew his name this time to be Morrison, not just a symbolic figure seen at dusk that first day. There was the same clearing in the forest, a kind of small tree. There she was, herself, looking on from behind the tree at the blonde girl and Morrison in the ungainly and beautiful throes of love. And there was the unbearable guilt.

For the blonde girl in the clearing making love to the big man was not Vicki, as she had supposed the other night.

Not Vicki at all.

It was herself.

Herself, as only she knew herself to be: a young woman who was still inside the middle-aged woman.

It was her in the clearing making the most vulgar and violent kind of love, and it was her, looking on. The woman hiding in the trees knowing guiltily the desire of her younger self in the meadow.

She should have known. She should have known that there were no favors in dreams. Morrison was for her, not for someone else.

There was no reason to call Vicki home. It was a mistake.

Oh, my love, I thought it had all died, all the feeling. But it lives. I live! Not only you can love, Vicki, my daughter.

In the darkness, Janet Harper wept.

The regret was real, for the hurt she had caused him in the drive to the factory that afternoon, for her tyranny. That such a man should be humiliated. Never again, she promised.

She thought: *Could I go to his room now?* But she knew she could not go to him this way. That would be *her* humiliation.

She wept into her pillow.

I'm a fool, she cried to herself. A young, young, young fool. Oh, love me....

Don't you think it's an odd trait, an odd choice? Of all the women in the group you could pair off with you chose a woman who is quite lovely but frigid as hell. I think I understand what your impulse is. You figure that a cold woman is the only one for you. You believe she'll be less demanding or not demanding at all, and that she'll feel less contempt for you. And with a frigid woman, you can always retaliate for failure and blame her for all your sexual fiascos. It's an interesting approach to your problem, but I'm sure you know it's not going to work.

CHAPTER 10

The smell of cigar smoke seemed built into the faded beige walls of Lieutenant Schwartz's office, a part of his old brown desk. All the men seated in the background of the light over his desk seemed to have always been there among the clinging odors. In the mouth of the lieutenant hung a cigar that, for the moment, took all the responsibility for years of work.

"Morrison," said Schwartz, "we've got to admit something to you. We're a bunch of foolish old men."

The group seated around the room watched the big man, content to allow Schwartz to speak for them.

"You understand by now that what all of us in this room have in common—except you, that is—no, even including you, Morrison, my friend—is that we want to get out from under that bitch named Janet Harper. And that means getting control of the business interest."

"I understand this in a general way," said Morrison cryptically.

"Good. A general way is the best way. You know about the report and all that stuff, don't you? Well, briefly, Ned Amsterdam was a sleuth, a private investigator who specialized in financial information. An accountant, a real operator. We hired him to look into the Harper business interests and find out what was wrong. He was supposed to deliver the report to one of us here, Ambrose Ford, who I'm sure you know."

"Yeah, I know him."

"To make the story short, Amsterdam was a cutie and tried to play both sides of the fence. The report was meant to show how poorly the widow lady is handling the vast business interest that we're all stockholders in. We intended to use the report as a weapon to unseat her at the next stockholders' meeting. But Amsterdam was fucking around and trying to find out what she'd pay to have the report delivered to her. So she sent someone out to pick up the report from him and teach the jerk a lesson about trying to squeeze a bitch for money; in other words, to beat the living shit out of Amsterdam. Whether she knew it or not that he'd get killed—because Bart Seely is a nut once he starts beating up on a guy—isn't really too important here. We'll get to Bart in our own good time, one way or another." Schwartz sighed. "The whole point is that what us old men want is to get control of the business, and the town, too, the way she has."

Morrison nodded.

"That doesn't mean we're bad old men," said the lieutenant, "or power-hungry or anything else that's nasty. We don't intend to misuse our powers. After all, we're already the leading citizens of the town and we're its logical power group. You already know Mr. Ford here, that's Carlotta's father, and our mortician Mr. Langley, and the doc and all the others—we're good citizens and we should be running those factories and this here town. We really should. But the lady doesn't see it that way. She keeps all the reins of power in her itsy bitsy fingers. Understand our problem?"

"I understand."

"Now when I say we're a bunch of foolish old men, I mean we've been mighty stupid about the way we tried to get around to the old lady. No, she's not so old, is she? That was an unfortunate adjective, under the circumstances. The circumstances were that in addition to the facts of the report to the stockholders of the corporation, we thought maybe we could get around her in the usual way a man does."

The police lieutenant looked around at his friends with a smile, accepted their return nods, then continued.

"So one by one we made our gentle plays for the town widow, and one by one we got shot down for our efforts. You see, we figured that if one of us could get to her, in a personal way, we could sort of lead her away from her unnatural and unfeminine role as the undisputed ruler of this business empire and the town that goes along with it. We figured, you might say, that if one of us could keep her occupied happily in the bedroom, she'd be more willing to forget what's going on at the office. But she not only turned down such overtures; she also threatened me and she told old Doc Sanders over there that if he ever so much as put his hand playfully on her fanny again, she would have him railroaded out of town or committed to the nearest lunatic asylum. She can do it, too, you'd better believe it!"

Morrison looked at the lieutenant levelly. "I don't see what any of this has to do with me," he said. "I'd rather not know all these things."

"Yes, I understand your point of view, young fellow, but we want you to know our problems. Because now you're going to help us."

Instinctively, the younger man moved back in his seat. The lieutenant chuckled.

"No need to get nervous. All we want is for you to get close to the nice lady."

"That's not possible," Morrison said sharply.

"Oh, I don't see why not. Do you see any problem with him getting close to the old lady, boys?" the policeman asked, turning his gaze from one to the other. The men in the room murmured their negative answer almost in unison.

"You're certainly a presentable young man," the lieutenant offered. "I mean, you're good-looking, you're built like Mr. America himself, and we just don't intend to see all these talents going to waste."

"The answer is no," said Morrison. "Mrs. Harper is not interested in me personally. I happen to know that."

"You sure?"

"I'm sure. Even if she were, I wouldn't—"

Schwartz held up a hand. "Let's not be too hasty to say what you would do and what you would not do. We're a pretty powerful group of people in this room, you know, and I wouldn't be in too much of a hurry to say no to people like us. We can do you a lot of good, son, but we can also be very unpleasant gentlemen."

Morrison shook his head helplessly. "I'm certain I could never influence Mrs. Harper in anything."

"Of course you can't—not if you continue calling her Mrs. Harper. Oh, I don't expect you to start acting familiar with her and calling her by her Christian name. Not yet. But when you're talking to us, man, you can call her Janet. We want you to. You've got to start thinking of her as an object of physical love."

The big man spoke tightly. "I told you gentlemen that the answer is no."

"We heard you. But we don't take that for an answer. I want to explain our plan to you, and then we'll listen to your objections. We agree that you probably won't be very successful at influencing Janet, even after you've been to bed with her. One of us older men might know how to make use of such a psychological advantage, but she's not going to be told what to do by a fellow your age."

The young man sighed. "I'm glad you see it that way."

"We're not unreasonable," the lieutenant insisted, as though hurt by the implication that they were. "We're not asking you to become her lord and master. All we want you to do is sleep with her. Now that's not such a tough assignment, is it? Christ, when I was your age...."

Morrison stared silently at the floor, shaking his head.

"Yes, that's the way it's going to be," said the lieutenant. "After you do it, we'll ship you off with enough cash so you'll be able to live in style for a good many years. Now that's a real fair bargain, isn't it?"

Eliciting no further response from the young man, he went on.

"We'll have no trouble getting everything arranged, but we do need your complete cooperation. Old Doc Sanders here can make sure the lady is given a dose of medicine— some kind of hallucinogen, I think you call it—so she won't resist your physical charms. That's easy enough for us to arrange. All you have to do is let nature take its course. And all we want to do is take pictures of the whole pretty scene. We've already decided where in her room to set up the cameras and the lights. She'll be under the influence of the LSD so she won't understand what's going on, and she'll never remember the details. All we want is some good footage of her going through the paces. No need for us right here to be vulgar about it or to explain what we need, right? We just want to have her on film, engaging in all the time-honored sexual acts that horny women are known for. Once we've got the film, she'll be a little more agreeable to our suggestions in the future. Now, all we ask of you...."

His voice trailed off as he and the others watched Morrison, whose face was buried in his hands, body sagging in defeat.

"What does this mean, boy?" Schwartz demanded.

"I can't," said Morrison. "I just can't."

They remained silent, waiting to hear the rest.

"I'm no good...with women."

"What the hell are you trying to tell us—that you're queer or something?"

"No. I'm impotent."

The doctor stood up and came forward. "You sure of that, son?"

Morrison smiled grimly. "I'm sure."

"Is it something physical or is it mental?"

"Mental," the big man said with a sigh. "At least that's what I've been told by every psychiatrist and therapist I've seen."

"Yes, it usually is." The doctor threw his hands up in the air. "It's no good, Jim."

"Like hell it's no good!" the lieutenant shouted. "He's lying. What the hell do you think he's been doing with that

Vicki bitch? You mean to say you haven't been laying that girl? You're lying." He turned to the other men. "Christ, it's got to be *him*, it's got to work with *him*, don't you understand? He's perfect. She dragged him in off the street, brought him to live at her place. Everybody in town figured he's been doing stud service for the old bag. She's in it up to her neck. She'd never be able to alibi the pictures if we can get them. Nobody'd ever believe that it was framed, and she'll know that nobody'd believe her. He's perfect."

The doctor shook his head sadly. "Jim, he's far from perfect."

The lieutenant, red-faced, glared at the young man as if he was about to jump up and strike him. He spoke between clenched teeth. "If you ever say a word about this meeting, Morrison...." Then he jerked his thumb toward the door. "Now get out!"

At the country club tennis court that afternoon, Carlotta was surprised by a visit from Janet, who was being chauffeured by old William. Mrs. Harper looked confused;

she looked as if she hadn't slept. She waited impatiently for Carlotta to finish, then they walked out to a private balcony that overlooked the golf course.

"I've been feeling bad about you," Janet said, touching Carlotta's hand tentatively. "I didn't really intend to make you look so cheap in front of Mr. Morrison."

Carlotta stared at the woman in astonishment. Janet's face showed concern. "You've been like a daughter to me, Carlotta," the woman went on. "After all, I took you under my wing."

"Why are you suddenly interested in Mr. Morrison's opinion of me?" the girl asked.

"It's simple. What I want—"

Carlotta's shoulders were stiff as she held to her hostility. "Tell me the real reason."

She waited, unrelenting in her angry stare, as Janet fumbled. Finally, the woman looked up at her beseechingly.

"It's Vicki.... I think Vicki's falling in love with him. That's not what I wanted."

Carlotta's throat was tight. "How do you know that?"

"I can tell. She's different."

The girl flared. "Well, what did you expect?"

"I didn't want that."

"Why not? Isn't he good enough for your pure, virginal daughter?"

"He's good enough to sleep with her," Janet said in a low, hoarse voice, "but I didn't want it going any further. I wanted him here so that Vicki could marry someone she could be proud of and not have to sleep around. You know how Vicki is. You understand...."

Carlotta looked away in disgust. Beyond the golf course, she traced the thick rim of trees, tall, beautiful trees that lined the driveway. She turned her gaze back to Janet Harper with a perverse feeling of triumph.

"Now your crazy plan has backfired. You tried to control everyone's life. Your children's. Mine. The lives of strangers. You have to control people; in fact, you're scared out of your wits if you can't control them. Well, you can do it to everyone, but not Vicki. She's an animal, always in heat, not even seasonal. And crazily enough, it gives her strength that the rest of us don't have. She won't care what you order her to do."

"You're wrong."

Carlotta continued without taking a breath. "If she loves him, she'll take him, maybe marry him, whether we like it or not."

"She can't!" Janet's face was flushed with shame. The confusion was there again in her eyes.

"You want him for yourself," Carlotta said. "You're thinking of using me now to break them up so you can have him yourself."

"Don't be ridiculous."

"Do you love him? Or do you just want him the way you say you want him for Vicki—as a man in bed?"

Janet lit a cigarette in an effort to control her agitation. "I don't know. I had a dream. The first evening I saw him in town, that night I dreamed he was with Vicki. But I dreamed it again, and it wasn't Vicki." She shook her head as if to shake out what lay hidden inside her. Her lips were contorted. "I'm a woman too! I didn't know my own mind. I had no idea I could desire—"

"Don't use that word!"

"That's what it is!" the older woman shouted, craning her head forward in emphasis. "You, you little passionless beauty—what do you know about desire? Well, I'm not like you. And I'm not too old, not really old at all. He's younger, but he's a real man. I never knew a real man. My husband was a fool and a weakling."

"What are you going to do?" the girl asked.

More in possession of herself now, Janet walked around the balcony, then swung her body toward Carlotta.

"I've told you more than enough," she said calmly. "I know what I want. No matter how ugly it may seem to you, the world doesn't only belong to the young and the beautiful. All women are driven, if they'd only admit it to themselves. I admit it. And I can do something about it. As for you!" Her stare turned cool. "You're right. It was a stupid thought, using you to break them up. You'll have nothing whatever to do with him. If I so much as catch you in a conversation with him, I'll bring the sky down on you and your family!"

She walked off slowly, as if she had merely come by for a friendly chat.

I'm generally against the use of drugs, but in a case of primary impotence, I think anything is worth trying. But if you're afraid of them, I understand, because I'm referring to the most daring drugs and any sensible man should be afraid of them. And I never ask a patient to try extreme remedies unless he asks for them first. What you must examine, however, is that your resistance to hypnosis and drugs is the fear you have when you're not in control of yourself...and that is certainly part of your problem, that fierce control you have over your own destiny.

CHAPTER 11

The need always came over Vicki with no warning. It came as a dull ache and as an angry gathering of nerves, like pulling a rubber band and waiting for it to break. Only it never broke until a man broke it for her.

There was no warning, and neither was there a stimulant. It did not come when she thought about a man, and not always when a man embraced or kissed her, nor did it always come when a man did any of the other things a man does to bring on the need in a woman. That was its own special way of coming on, but this was more spontaneous and demanding. It came unheeded and it had nothing to do with a man or his thoughts or the state of the world.

Sometimes, however, it was only a slight ache and she could overcome it. That had happened, she remembered, when she got off the plane and rode in the car for the first time with Morrison. But that had been enough. She was glad it hadn't been a grand attack because she would not have wanted him to see her that way. True, he thought of her as a tramp. But he hadn't personally seen her as the animal she was now.

Yet, what of now? What time was it—three, four in the morning? She pictured Morrison before her, seated on the bed, and her hands reached out for him, her body quivering. She was beginning to perspire and it made her cold. She leaped from the bed and put on her robe. Quietly, she opened her door.

When she came to in front of his room, she suddenly felt afraid. Was she now going to ruin everything? She opened his door without knocking.

He sat up quickly, bare to the waist, his enormous chest and shoulders outlined in the soft moonlight. A cry that was a whimper escaped from her lips. She ran to the bed and held him as though he could save her from the thing that was drowning her. He tried to hold her off, but she would not release her arms from around his neck. There was an amazing strength in those soft arms. Finally, he put his arm around her as she continued to cling to him and rub her body against the hardness of his chest in a side-to-side motion. He let her do it, then held her off, gripping her shoulders. Her head fell loosely forward and her golden hair brushed his forearms. He was breathing heavily.

"Please control yourself, Vicki. I'm not going to do it."

She lifted her head. Her eyes were fogged, unbelieving. "Not going to do it?" She bared her teeth and half-laughed. "Of course you're going to do it!"

"No," he said calmly.

"YES!" Her body sprang forward and knocked him back on the pillow. She jumped up and straddled his legs. He reacted with incredible speed. She didn't know anyone could move that fast. In the flash of a second, she had been thrown into the air, caught in one of those powerful arms, then her face met with a short, restrained blow from one of his broad hands.

"You didn't understand me?" he asked tightly.

"But why?" she sobbed.

He held her at arm's length, his face darkly angry. "Because I don't want to, that's why."

"Morrison, I—I love you. Please let me tell you how I love you!"

"Vicki, I'm sorry. I'm not the right man for you."

"But why wouldn't you be?" she insisted. "Why do you want to make me find another man when you know it's you I want?"

"Don't feel that way about me. I'm not staying here very long. I may cut out any day."

"You're leaving? Why?"

They stood in the middle of the room and he looked at her sadly. "Why? You ought to ask why I haven't left before this. How long did you expect me to go on being a male call girl?"

"You're not any such thing," she said, moving closer to stroke his chest. He caught her arm. "Mother'll do it if I don't," she said nastily. "Anyway, if you try to leave, she'll have you picked up on some charge and take you back on good conduct. She'd really strangle you then."

"No harm in trying," he said reasonably. "This isn't exactly my idea of a man's life. Better off being a fugitive."

"But what about me?" Vicki cried.

"What about you?"

"I want to go with you."

"What kind of game is this?"

"No game. I'm in love with you. You must know that, right?"

He smiled dimly. "Then I'm sorry I can't return the feeling. I guess I've got fixed ideas about what the girl I want has to be like."

"Girl??" Vicki drew away. "How like you to say 'girl.' I'm talking about a man and a woman, not a boy and a girl. What do you call your idea of what a girl should be like? Your Dream Girl? Your Ideal Girl? You're talking like a kid and here I'm offering you a woman's love."

"Cut it out!" he said. She was touching something very sore.

"Is Carlotta your idea of a 'girl'?" she taunted.

"You're damn right."

"Ha! Would she fight for you? Would she give up everything for you? No, she wouldn't."

"Yes," he said. "I'm going to ask her to come with me—out of this damn town."

The silence was like a mountain in the room. Vicki stepped back. "I don't believe you," she said.

He didn't answer.

"She hasn't got the guts to give everything up, to cross my mother," Vicki murmured, as if to herself.

"We'll see."

"Have you asked her yet?" Her voice was cold, distant.

"No...I—it'll take a little time."

"You're a fool, Morrison. You want to throw yourself away on a piece of ice who wouldn't have the nerve—she'll never make you happy, you big jerk!"

His reply was almost inaudible. "I have to try, Vicki."

Without another word, she turned and left the room.

Only later did she realize that, in her jealousy and anger, the need for sex had entirely deserted her.

Yes, you're genitally drawn to your own mother. You don't dare succeed with any woman because that would mean you would fornicate with your own mother and you can't face that. You were so guilty about how you wanted your mother that you anesthetized your body, made it a tomb.

So what if you slept in your mother's bed. So what if she played with you once or maybe more than once. What the hell. Maybe she was drunk. Don't let it ruin you. You've heard of women who are so shocked on their wedding night by their husband's lack of finesse that they turn away from sex from then on. Well, that's what your mother did to you, young man; she gave you the wedding night blues for the rest of your life.

CHAPTER 12

Mr. Morrison to see you, ma'am," the maid said.

Carlotta's dark head started from her pillow. A pulse leaped into her throat. The maid stood waiting, her face registering curiosity at the girl's confusion.

"I'm—I'm not well enough to receive visitors," Carlotta began. "Tell him I can't—"

His footsteps entering the room cut her short. The maid shrugged and walked from the room, closing the door behind her. Silence followed her exit.

Finally, Carlotta made herself look up at the tall man standing full against the closed door. He was staring at her in bed as though drinking her in. She felt naked. With an old maid's gesture, she pulled the covers up to her neck. A smile flickered momentarily on his face.

She wondered why he didn't say something. The situation was awkward, embarrassing, almost unreal. Her own horizontal position, adding to his impression of height, made her feel as though she were looking up at someone from the bottom of a well. She could feel herself sinking as the uninvited man advanced across the room.

"How are you feeling this morning?" he asked in a gentle voice. He seemed to be holding back a flood of other things he wanted to say.

"Not well," she whispered.

He took another step closer. She cringed, wondering with astonishment if he was going to lean over and take her in his arms. But he stopped short of touching her and looked down at her.

Her shoulders relaxed. She appraised him coolly. *That's better*, she thought; *he had me frightened there for a moment*. The physical presence of the man! *Thank God*, she breathed, *I'm not carried away by things like that*.

"Will you have a seat," she said, patting the bedclothes beside her. Then she gasped at her unconscious gesture. "I— I mean, why don't you have a chair?"

"Sure." He picked up her tufted wingback chair and deposited it near the bed. Then he lowered himself so carefully into it that she had to smile, but only for a second.

"Are you here with a message from Mrs. Harper? Or is it from Vicki?"

"Neither," he said, smiling uncertainly. "I wanted to visit you."

"I'm rather ill," she offered tiredly. "If there's nothing important...." she let her voice trail off.

"Not too ill to receive a mere visitor, I hope," he said, half in concern, half in sarcasm.

"Yes, I am, actually."

"You're a bad liar," Morrison said sharply.

She waited in shocked silence. He rose from the chair and loomed over her.

"Yes, you're lying," he repeated, and she felt herself paralyzed from her neck to the end of her body. She wondered vaguely if her mouth wasn't agape and she tried to swallow.

"You're not in the least ill," he continued in a tighter voice. "You've been trying to avoid me. You know that I've been trying to see you. And this whole sick act—I'll bet it has something to do with not seeing me. Well, I never knew a lady to go to such extremes before. What are you scared of, Carlotta?"

She found her voice and it was strong. "Will you please go!"

"Listen," he said earnestly, leaning forward a bit. "I know you're afraid. I can tell. In front of other people, you're—well, you're always looking around as if you're scared to get caught with me. But that wasn't the way it was the first time I saw you, was it? We communicated something then, didn't we?"

"That's not true," she said weakly, turning her face away.

"Look at me," he demanded. "We're man and woman now. There's no one else here. You don't have to worry about who sees you with me. And don't hem and haw. I want straight talk. This is important to me."

"I think I'll ring for the maid now," she said coldly.

"You do and I'll throw her out."

She fell back on her pillow, forgetting this time to draw the covers up to her neck. She had no idea how to handle this situation. There had never been a time she could not dismiss a man or attain the upper hand. Because of his very size, perhaps, this man defeated her. And yet, instinctively and out of her defeat, she took the one attitude that could be disconcerting to him.

"I'm sorry," she said wearily, "that you've read so much into my behavior. Apparently, you've deluded yourself into thinking that I was...interested in you. I apologize if I gave any indication of such interest."

It was a stiff, almost bookish speech, and for a moment, his eyes clouded doubtfully. His lips tightened and he fought off the doubt.

"I know I'm right. I've thought about it too much. I don't usually suffer from delusions. No, I'm not going to let it rest at that, Miss Ford."

"How—what—" Panic rose in Carlotta's voice. "I don't understand."

"You understand."

There was sureness in his voice. Her face was deathly white, as though her feigned sickness had suddenly come to pass. After a pause in which she seemed to be assembling some inner energy, she spoke softly.

"I believe you've done what you came to do. You came to frighten me, and now I'm frightened."

"Frighten you? Of all things! I came on an errand of happiness. That's what it meant to me. I suppose I was wrong, though."

"Yes. You'd better leave."

"I could have sworn—" he started. Then he sighed. "You must consider me some kind of stupid oaf."

"Please leave!" she groaned, as if in pain.

Her overreaction puzzled him. There was more in her cry than an exit cue. He bent his head down over hers. Her gray-green eyes were wide with fear, her lips trembling with helplessness and yet anticipation. Slowly, his mouth lowered to meet hers. It was a passionless kiss on his part, a mere test. When her lips opened and began to drink hungrily from him, they did so without the girl's conscious permission.

She remained still, eyes closed, as he moved back and stood above her once again. His voice floated in through a haze.

"That's all I wanted to know," he said.

Her throat let out a noiseless sob.

He went on relentlessly. "You can't hide in your sickbed forever. I'll be waiting when you step out."

She gazed up at him. "I'm not worth waiting for. There's nothing inside. I know I'm beautiful. But that's all there is."

"No, I see a lot more than that," he said. "I'm asking you to believe that there's a beautiful you under the other person. A warm, feeling person."

She shook her head. "You need to understand what I'm trying to say."

"I understand, but I refute it."

"Then you don't know me," she went on tiredly. "It's not just a matter of my being cold or even passionless. It's that there's a complete vacuum under the exterior. That's the thing about me. That's why sometimes even I'm fascinated by myself, by my own face, my own body. Sometimes I stare into the mirror. Not because I'm so vain or egotistical but because I'm trying to find the secret of why I appear so beautiful, why everyone else sees a real person in that beauty when I know it isn't so."

Once again, he refused to accept this. "You're confusing many different things, Carlotta. There can be specific reasons you don't feel passion as quickly as the next person. You have to give yourself time to learn how to love, how to feel. Don't you understand—we're perfect for each other. Because I need time, too."

She frowned at him suddenly, puzzled. "What do you mean?"

"I mean—" He swallowed, embarrassed. "Damn it, I'm a lot like you, that's all. I'm all...bottled up inside. It's not easy for me to let myself go any more than it is for you."

"Morrison, you don't really get what I mean."

"Oh yes I do," he insisted. "I have the same problem. I need time and I need a chance to adjust. So do you. That's one reason we'd be perfect for each other. Don't you see? We could teach each other." He observed the way she was staring at him.

"I love you," he said earnestly. "That's what I've been waiting for, to love someone. Now I've got something to start with. Up to now, my relationships have been purely impersonal and mechanical. But I guess I'm not made that way." He bent forward and took her hands in his. "You're the same way, I can tell. You can't just be a mechanical person; you've got to have a basic attraction. You feel that for me, don't you?"

"Yes, you're an attractive man, all right."

"Then let's try to reach each other—because nobody will be able to do it for us. We can only do it for each other. Please, Carlotta."

"Do you think you can reach me?"

"I'm sure of it. Don't be afraid. Just have patience. And faith."

"I'm too afraid."

"Good. That means you think I'm going to touch a part of your nature that you haven't allowed anyone to come near."

"You're not lying to me, are you?" she implored. "You *do* need me—in the same way I need you?"

"More than you know," he sighed. "There's nothing keeping us apart, except maybe Janet Harper. And I don't want you to be afraid of her. We're beating her, you know."

The girl's puzzlement was written on her brow. "I don't understand how you can say that."

"Think about it. That whole thing with Nelly. She was trying to change our minds about each other, trying to make you look bad in my eyes. Before, she didn't care what we thought. She just gave orders."

Carlotta smiled wryly. "She can still give orders. Nothing's changed."

"She's changed. She's gone soft. I can tell."

The girl looked at him with knowing eyes. "She's gone head over heels in love with you, that's where she's gone."

"Are you serious?!"

She nodded. "I'm sure. She made it quite plain that she's now courting you on her own behalf, not Vicki's."

"Why, the old goat!" He laughed. "So that's why she's losing her bite!"

"I wouldn't count on her losing anything. Maybe it's made her a little less sure of herself; maybe it's thrown her off-balance for the moment, but it's only for the moment."

"Then, for Chrissake, let's seize the moment. Let's get the hell out of this town while she's off-balance."

"Get out? Where to?"

"Let's get out of the state. Elope."

Carlotta's eyes registered shock as they looked into his. Then she looked away. "We'd probably never get out of here," she said.

"Then we don't have to leave the state. You know that. We could shoot over to Jefferson for a few days and get a Justice of the Peace. And by the time they find out where we are, we'd be old married folks." He held up his hand. "No, don't interrupt. Think of it this way. Once we're married, what can she do? She'd make a fool of herself if she tried to annul the marriage just so she could have me. There'd be no salvaging the situation for herself."

"I don't know. I can't think straight while you're with me." Carlotta closed her eyes. "I think you should go. I promise to think about it, but please don't stay anymore."

When she opened her eyes again, he was gone.

Why are you letting a woman get ahead of you on line? Aren't you stronger than she is? I said LINE UP in the order of power and dominance. Aren't you more dominant than a mere female? Knock her out of the way. Touch her, don't be afraid. Go touch their genitals, any one of them. Pick a woman. Now go down on her. Eyeball the crotch, examine her, let's stop treating this like it's the Temple of the Gods. Get in there and eat it....

CHAPTER 13

Well, Mother," said Lance, waving his glass of amber liquid back and forth in front of his eyes, "you've saved your son from a fate worse than death. Always saving me from something, aren't you? Since I was a kid, you've been convinced I can't fight my own battles."

Janet looked with resignation at the glass in his hand and settled into a wicker chair across from him in the sunroom.

"Now you've saved me from little Nelly," he said. "You've held court and Nelly's been convicted as a liar and a rapist. Well, you know something, I've got a goddamn notion to marry that girl."

Mrs. Harper flinched, and he smiled at the effect of his announcement. Her hand drummed impatiently on the arm of her chair. "If I had the energy, I would get up and slap your face for that," she said.

The smile left his face. Sourly, he gulped a mouthful of his drink.

"Yes, I'd slap your face," she went on. "You were always a coward, and I've always had to protect you."

"And you always called me a coward to make sure I became one."

"Lance, it didn't take any effort on my part to make a coward of you. Let's not blame me."

He shrugged. "I guess you're right, then."

"Of course I am. Your trouble has been that you're too much of a weakling to admit your weaknesses. Well, I should have allowed Nelly to blackmail you into marriage. Don't think it didn't cross my mind! But I was soft and I was a mother. A mother protects her son against lying, scheming women. But I should have let her take you. You deserve to be married to an ugly, stupid girl, a girl you couldn't possibly love."

"And who says I couldn't? A man can love an ugly girl," he said airily.

She chuckled. "You think so? Some men, yes, but not you. You don't know how to love. Men like you end up marrying the most beautiful girl who will have them. That's the extent of what most men can love: someone they can show off to the world. I'd just like to see you with an ugly girl. You'd die of shame."

Tears sprang to his eyes. "You never taught me to love. You never gave me enough strength or anything. That's why I'm the way I am. That's why Vicki—"

"Oh, shush. I can't tolerate this sniveling."

"Neither can I," he whispered.

"Then stop the nonsense. No more talk about Nelly. The girl lied. She's probably afraid she'll never get married, so she's trying to get as many men in any way she can. She lied about sleeping with you. And if she didn't lie, then it's the same thing, because she slept with a drunken fool who couldn't even defend himself and who can't even remember it. Do you think I'd let you marry a girl you slept with and forgot you slept with? Oh no. You wouldn't have forgotten if you slept with Carlotta."

"Don't start that stuff again, Mother."

Janet nodded craftily. "Didn't you think she was available?"

He shook his head.

"You'd like to sleep with her, wouldn't you? You'd even like to marry her."

His eyes filled with pain. "She's so beautiful. But you make me hate myself."

"Lance, don't hate yourself for that," she said, her own eyes softening. "All men are weaklings and fools about beauty. Almost all," she added. "There isn't a man in this town who wouldn't want to go to bed with Carlotta. Not one married man in this town would have married his present wife if he could have had Carlotta Ford as his wife. That's the way men are. A man's love is a meaningless thing. A woman wins a man when he can't win a more beautiful woman. There isn't one marriage I know of that could survive if some beautiful Hollywood star were to get it into her head that she wanted the husband." She took a breath and leaned back into her chair. "And you're no different. I think that you might be better than most men because you've got a conscience. You hate yourself, at least; you're not really more of a weakling than they are, just more honest. So why shouldn't you have what they all want?" Janet continued. "Why shouldn't you marry the most beautiful girl in this town, possibly in this state? Yes, you'll be proud that you've got the prettiest. You're going to enjoy her and feast on her and ravage her—"

"Oh, Mother, please," he said calmly. "You mean that I'm going to marry Carlotta whether she wants to or not. But why should it make any difference to you if I want to marry Nelly instead?"

"Because why take the worst when you can have the best?"

"All right." His shoulders sagged.

Janet stood and walked to the door, opening it without turning to look at him, and left.

He stared at the door, then put his bottle on the table in front of him, staring at it. Then he leaned his face over the table and kissed it. He'd meant to shrug off the whole scene the way he usually did, but it wouldn't work today. A wave of depression was upon him. Somehow, he couldn't stay here, and he couldn't reach for another drink. He'd be drinking all night at the club dance, so it was best to slow down now.

He stared at the bottle and felt pity for all those drinkers in all those corners of the earth who were continuously cut off, always threatened with the horror of being cut off from this juice of life. Yet he could feel no need to leap at this bottle and gulp it down as he had seen so many men do because there were always bottles for him and would always be bottles for him... as long as he didn't offend his mother.

He left the sunroom in a philosophical mood. He walked into town and up the steps of Nelly's house. He had to talk to her. He felt that he'd failed her. He wanted to tell her he didn't want to fail her.

Nelly's mother, looking at him strangely, told him that her daughter was in her room.

"She's packing," the woman called after him as he began to ascend the steps.

A dry-eyed Nelly opened the door to his knock.

"Come in, Lance," she said, very much as if she had expected him.

He entered and looked around the room. A blue suitcase lay open on the bed and garments were strewn in the classical manner of hurried packing.

"I think I knew that you'd be leaving," he said.

"There's a lot to do," she offered conversationally. "I won't be able to leave until late tonight. I may even catch an early morning train."

"Where are you going?"

"An aunt in Chicago," she answered blandly.

There was a knock at the door. Nelly's mother stuck her head in.

"Do you need any help packing?" her mother asked. What she meant, Lance thought, was, "Do you need me to protect you from this drunkard you so unwisely love?"

"No thank you," the girl said, then she waited until her mother's footsteps could be heard on the stairs before she turned her gaze back to the room. She didn't look at Lance directly as she advanced toward the bed. "I have to hurry—" she began.

"Why do you have to leave?" he cried suddenly.

She stopped. Her shoulders stiffened defensively.

"You don't have to go," he pleaded.

"Yes, I do," she responded calmly. "You see, I've made what they call a mess of things. I tried and failed. Hand me some of those clothes, please."

Lance reached for the white garments on the far side of the bed to hand her. When he realized he was holding Nelly's underwear, he became confused. She took them from him quickly.

"I guess it's stupid of me to be embarrassed touching your clothes after what happened between us."

Nelly's face became red under her freckles.

"I'm sorry," he said.

"Nothing happened between us, Lance. Do you understand that?"

"Yes," he said.

"And forget what I said to your mother about loving you. I was lying."

"You don't lie, Nelly."

She shook her head vigorously. "I do, I do."

"No. You're just forgiving me," he said.

"There's nothing to forgive. Everything's my fault. I've always, well, I've always felt...."

"Have you always loved me?" he asked, disbelieving. "Even when we were kids?"

"I've always wanted to take care of you; that's what it was. I somehow always figured that I would be the one to take care of you. I don't understand why. It was silly, I guess. Just because I wanted it so much was no reason to think that I'd get what I wanted. But for some reason, I thought you'd someday want me, too. Maybe because I knew there was no one else who wanted to take care of you. There may be women who love you, but they won't feel the way I do."

He let out a breath. "No other women love me. There's no one else who wants me. Not really. I could be a better man than I am, you know; all I needed was someone who believed in me."

"I always did."

"I know. At least I know it now...now, when you're leaving." He started toward her. "Nelly, I don't say I've changed, and I don't say I've suddenly fallen in love with you. It's just that I see you differently than I used to. I didn't lie when I said that I didn't remember anything about that night. But I know what it must have taken you to do what you did. And I realize what you sacrificed—especially in pride."

"What's the purpose of you coming here, Lance?"

"I want you to stay. I want you to give us time to know each other in a different way than we used to. I want to make you forget all the things I've done in the past, the embarrassment and the jokes my friends and I made at your expense."

Tears showed in her eyes. "It's strange that when someone offers to be good to you, that's when you start to cry." She laughed girlishly. "No, it's no good. We can't change ourselves because we want to. You're not going to fall in love with me just because you think you should. And don't forget your mother. She'd never allow us to see each other. She has other plans for you."

"I suppose I was just talking...or hoping. But you'll leave on tomorrow morning's train and I'll go on the way I did before. Or I'll marry Carlotta and it'll be something to be proud of, the way my mother says it will, but I'll still be lost."

Nelly turned away. "Goodbye, Lance."

He walked to the door. "Will you be coming to the club dance tonight?"

"No, I won't have time."

"Then goodbye, Nelly. I'll drink a toast to you tonight."

Slowly, the door closed and he was gone.

Maybe your physical symptoms are only a means of avoiding other kinds of hurts and dangers that aren't physical. Maybe you're saying, "Look at me, I'm impotent, so please don't ask anything of me...don't expect anything of me...don't hurt me emotionally..."

Those powerful arms and shoulders, that proud carriage of your head. Don't you realize that your ego is situated almost entirely in the upper half of your body? Your pelvis and legs are the forgotten territories. Loosen your body so that feelings can flow through it. You've stopped all feelings from reaching your sexual organs. Impotence is a holding back, an asthma of the gonads.

CHAPTER 14

Bart Seely was the first one at the country club dance to feel the effects of the free-flowing liquor. The circular bar and the ballroom began tilting and spinning at such a frightening rate that he ran out to the garden for air, only to run headlong into a more limitless terror. Here he faced nothing but the expansive, uncaring firmament. The sky was the wrong place to look, that vault of heaven. It told the whole story of his puny self that he feared to know. It was the place to fear, the hinterland of a lifelong nightmare, the place that would not forget murder and guilt. Would he ever shake the image of that murdered man? Oh, how he wished that he could revert to some religious or primitive philosophy for a knowledge of safety! Wouldn't it be comforting to warm himself with the belief in the enclosed universe, that large, velvet-lined tabernacle the ancients thought the sky to be? But he knew that all was emptiness, that the earth certainly was no haven; that if you cross-sectioned this miserable planet with a sharp edge, it would be nothing but the insides of a baseball, ragged rubber and string, batted around the universe, out of shape.

And each man...each man had the same senseless ending and the same crazy-yawning universe to contend with. For each man it was strictly the Lindbergh bit: he did it all on his own. Which was the beauty of it all, he used to think when he was younger. Hadn't he always prided himself on his manliness and need for no one? But no longer. Murder had ruined him.

He was off the terrace now, circling the gardens, full of panic. Darkness. The country club's main building loomed as though it breathed; massive, rocklike, incredible rock upon rock in the face of this globular spinning in a senseless vacuum built by men who did not know the enormity of their presumptuousness.

He heard the footsteps of a pair of lovers and he dodged, hurrying along the quickset hedge that paralleled the balustrade, and he jumped down to the far railing along the side. There, on the porch, he saw the young man brilliantly lit from the window, drinking directly from the bottle of whiskey.

"What the hell do you want?" Lance scowled.

Bart tried to smile. It had a sickly look. "Now, come on, Lance, don't get so unfriendly."

"Ha. What's this, you're suddenly a friend?"

"Sure," he said, just to talk to someone until his panic subsided. "Sure, I'm your friend. I never had anything against you. I like you."

"Go fuck yourself."

"Lance, I gotta ask you a question. Promise me you won't laugh. But I have to ask."

"I don't feel like laughing."

Bart remained silent.

"Well," said Lance, looking at him indolently, "ask your damn question. Ask it and then split."

"You've got to promise me," said Bart.

"What? That I won't laugh? No, I won't laugh."

"Not only that. Promise me you won't ever tell anybody what I asked you."

This request brought the blond head up with some interest. "All right. What is it?"

"Well, the thing I want to know is—now, don't get me wrong—I just want to know, conversationally, you know what I mean. Lance, have you ever had anything to do with a man?"

"What the hell are you talking about?"

"Don't get me wrong. I just wondered if maybe you...?"

"Why the hell are you asking that?"

"I don't know."

"Bart, you son of a bitch, are you queer?"

Bart shook his head slowly but said nothing.

"Are you?" Lance persisted.

The powerful man breathed deeply of the sharp night air, his head bowed.

"Say it!" Lance demanded.

"I—I don't know," said Bart. "I keep thinking about it."

"About me?"

"Sometimes."

Lance started to giggle. "What is it you want? You want to eat me or something?"

Bart was now glaring at him. "Fuck you, you bastard." Then, as if realizing he said the wrong thing, he stepped back.

"Come closer," said Lance with a conciliatory smile.

"No," said Bart. "I—that's not—"

"Come here, that's all."

Bart stared. He saw that his old friend, his old enemy, was opening his fly and laughing, offering it, offering it. A cry of rage broke free from Bart's throat. He struck out at Lance again and again, feeling the warm blood on his hands as the young man's face sank in and his moaning body fell like a limp rag doll.

Whatever you learn, you must learn yourself. "What comes in through the gate is not family treasure" is what the Chinese say. So your instincts are right—leave it all and discover yourself. Forget your civilized accomplishments, forget you're an engineer and go somewhere to work with your hands. Too many of us use our professions as a badge of prestige to wall ourselves off from the daily battle and from other people. Carry no labels with you.

CHAPTER 15

What the hell is happening, Morrison asked himself. He'd felt peculiar right after dinner. They were supposed to drive to the club later for that shindig, where he intended to ask Carlotta again if she would leave with him, and he told Mrs. Harper he wanted to rest awhile, which she said was a good idea because she also wanted to take a nap. But now he felt dizzy, kind of seasick. The goddamn bed was rocking like a boat. And the light. Here it was long past sundown and he was afraid to open his eyes.

Lids tightly shut, he propped himself up a few inches on the pillow and cautiously unsquinted. The light was pitiless. More lights outside the windows were there to scare away burglars and they were like suns, each shipping four million tons of illumination per second, all of it into his room. The room was burning up with light, humming light, singing light, shimmering light. The metal bedposts proclaimed it and smiled like toothpaste ads; the furniture outlined it as if auditioning for a Vermeer masterpiece; the walls spread themselves shakily before it. He felt a reasonless, causeless giggle within himself as the men appeared.

Amid strange distortions of objects on all sides of him like reflections in a doorknob they appeared, three or four men in the doorway. Light poured from behind them and they filled the doorway, glistening like salt miners emerging from their labors. Their eyes were poetic sunsets; they were naked as the day they were born. Colorful lights streamed in past them as from behind religious figures in an old etching. They were in water up to their knees, naked in water. "Let's take him now," they said.

He became terrified, for the room was filling with water. Up, up, over his head. They had hold of him under the water and were tugging at him. Lieutenant Schwartz, the doctor, Carlotta's father, the other whose name he forgot. They came to him in the watery depth of his half-dream. He felt nothing; his body, the bedclothes, the floor he walked on nakedly, the air itself—all were an impalpable part of the sloshing, buoyant texture. Shadows hung over him as they pulled him from the room; the light played its spectrum game happily, as if it had found on his lids a spiderweb in a meadow...here and there a whorl, now and again some calcareous substance from their world to his. The lieutenant and his friends were naked, milky flounders, wavering faces made of alabaster. "I hope," said one, "that we didn't give him too much." Half-floating as he was, they circled and led him down the hall, their words coming out in separate bubbles, all friendly words under the water, words of encouragement, encouragement for what he knew not....

They floated toward Mrs. Harper's room, their voices booming, then fading—as if some terrible god were controlling the volume. Designs in the hall rug quivered under his step like shrinking starfish trapped in a reddish haze. As the men spoke, he had the extraordinary realization that if they were to blow into one of his ears, like into a musical instrument, beautiful chords would come blaring out his other ear. The water was becoming heavier and heavier, like molasses, almost impossible for them to swim through, darker as it grew thicker. Only with the greatest effort could he lift his arms or bend his knees to swim toward the new light. They went through the door into the room and he blinked at the shock of new lights, big lights, lights singing and crashing through the green and purple thickness. There were men behind the lights, naked men. "There he is, get the camera on him!" said someone. He saw Janet Harper, pink in her nakedness, her mouth opening and closing. "Snakes! Snakes!" she was screaming. Her naked skin glowed youthfully, glowed forth from the bed on which she lay, her breasts zooming forward, largely, pinkly, then retreating into a laughing, tinkling sound of distant music.

"Snakes, snakes, get them away!" she was screaming in terror, shrinking against the pillow. Everything she said, every sound, had the alarming effect of upsetting the environment, causing chairs and lights in her room to float away while his own movement attracted objects—the furniture attached to his moving limbs by invisible strings—and everything was glowing in and out....

Yet he was still in the water and had to get out of the water. He had always been here. Incredible to have been here all his life and not even know it; this protective, womblike world. Forever in the water. No wonder he was soft and had no power. If he could only get his body out of the water...it was only just above his head...if he could reach up, climb out. Now, now. With all his strength, he lifted himself but barely moved inches in the thick, molasses-like sea. He could feel coolness on his forehead where his head had topped the water.

One of the men offered a hand to help him up, but he recoiled when he perceived in horror that the man's hand was made up of five penises surrounding, in its palm, a moist, throbbing vagina. He brushed it away and fought his way up. He was breathing air, not quite out of the sea to his chin, his face turning to stone as it met the air, like one of Rodin's sculptures, trapped half-in and half-out, barely above the level of suffocation. With superhuman effort, he fought his way out of the waterstone, chinning out, lifting himself by bulging biceps, then—hands-free—pulling one leg out, then the other.

Get it up! they were shouting jubilantly. *That's it…get it up!*

He was out of the water. He heard their gasps and murmurs. He was on his feet, being pushed toward the bed. Janet was screaming *Snakes! Snakes!* and he was embarrassed that his penis was still made of rock and rose so large before him. He had the terrible fear that his enormous member would turn in its large fierceness, and, in an act of suicidal madness, would attack its owner and club him to death.

He was pushed forward and now Janet's breasts were slapping against him. She clung to him. He thrust her away, straddled her and stared at her. Then he grasped her breasts and kneaded them while she groaned, whether in pain or anger or pleasure he could hardly say and didn't care. His body was rock, all of it cold except for the large member extended before him that was glowingly warm, then on fire, seeking to be quenched. With a cry of triumph, he mounted her as the lights came closer and naked bodies crowded around the bed. He heard her sob of joy and her grotesque endearments as he plunged into the hot wetness again and again...would it never end? Then came the gushing warmth from inside his loins spilling into the body that was convulsing beneath him. Her screams were deafening as she held to him, her bracelets jangling cold on his back, her nails digging into his flesh. Then she turned into a black cat and was licking his body, then was on top of him, his member inside her again, then she was licking once more and trying to swallow him and exhaust his hardness, which refused to go soft. Then again he was on top and the woman whose legs were wrapped around him was his mother and he plunged into her viciously. *Too much*, said a soft voice from afar, one of the men. "Get him off her. She's had too much. Diane, you're going to have to help out."

"I said no. I put the stuff in the food. That was all I was supposed to do."

"Do what you're told. Get those clothes off or do we have to rip them off?"

"He can kill someone."

"We'll watch for him, for Chrissake."

"Then get the old bitch out of here. And no cameras."

"All right, no cameras."

Do you know that a baby will die or go completely insane if he does not have social interaction? Think of it—die. It makes no difference that he is well-fed and kept warm in some kind of box. If he doesn't hear voices or feel touch or have some contact with others, he will simply go berserk or die off.

Now this tells us something. No person is wholly responsible for his own will to live, for his own energy or motivation. These things are fed to us by others. We must interact, bounce off others all the time. It is all there waiting for you; you have merely to connect, to extend yourself. Meet one person above all others; you've got to like a woman, not fear her or hate her or want to overcome her or anything else. Not even necessarily love her; you must like her as a person.

CHAPTER 16

He left the Harper house feeling nothing at all about Diane or about the men who were still restraining Janet. He understood why the men had done it and felt no rancor. They, in turn, saw no reason to try to stop him from getting dressed—or perhaps they didn't dare get in his way physically now that he was coming out of it. In his pocket, he found the keys to the limousine that he had chauffeured so often. He drove into the night toward the country club, lighting up the trees with the powerful beams. Up there was the moon in its third quarter, at right angles to an unseen sun. He was still not out of his drug-induced state of removal from himself; he visualized the moving car as something being watched as it rode swiftly by a god with a long, black telescope.

Now I know how Juliana felt, he said to himself, Juliana of Retinnes, a martyr and saint he once learned about from his religious and half-demented mother. Juliana, he recalled, was saying her prayers one night and she saw a vision of a beautiful moon that had a piece broken off. She implored God to explain what it meant. God told her it meant nothing. Probably that was the most devastating and extraordinary thing God ever told anybody: that something meant nothing, that there is no answer, that it is all a box within a box within a box....

He reached the country club driveway where the most majestic trees of all loomed before the car: tall shadows genuflecting to the powerful headlights. He got out of the car and stood like an alert animal catching the sound of music from the club band as an animal catches scent, unable to move. He didn't know *why* he had come, for which one. All the way here, he had taken it for granted that he was hurrying to fetch Carlotta, to take her away from this life, but now, he hesitated because he knew it was a past impulse being acted upon out of an old logic.

Two young men went by into the club, into the music, and they stopped their conversation long enough to glance at him in a hesitant, friendly fashion as though unsure whether they knew him or not. He felt a certain strength of kinship with them. He was one of them. He was proud to be one of them, one of millions, billions.

A trembling began in his body and sweat broke out on his face, cooled by the night breeze. He admitted something basic about himself, that he'd always felt apart from other men because of his affliction, that he'd wanted nothing in life but to be as ordinary as other men. Ordinary meant supreme. Oh, yes, he'd know that he had always envied them, but he rarely admitted *how much* he'd envied them. Only now, when it seemed he had no more reason to envy anyone, could he admit that want and failure had been killing him since the day he first recognized that he was an afflicted man.

And now? He wasn't sure what all the factors were that separated him from the past. If it meant drugs from here on in, so be it. He was certain, however, that he'd never have to rely on them, that he glimpsed the possibilities of infinite boundaries and discovered a new self. He learned that there was less terror in being without boundaries than he had supposed. He had indeed been afraid to be himself.

Now, in a strange way, he was more of a man and less of an individual; that was it; that was why he'd felt that kinship with his male contemporaries as they walked by. He listened to a woman's laugh from within the party. *Let's go*, he said to himself.

He walked quickly up the steps to a tall, slim, unknown girl who stood in the doorway. As the light fell on him, she emitted a low whistle. "Well, come on in, handsome."

Then he was inside, past her—the girl's confidential and inviting voice following him—past the long circular bar, along the red-paneled walls and the rich Florentine paintings, into the area where the plush easy chairs and lounges were scattered. His gaze found the contour of Vicki's blonde head and lovely white shoulders peeking from behind one of the chairs. She was talking earnestly to a seated group of men and women who all seemed well on their way to intoxication.

He walked to the group and stood behind her. The perfume she wore, which he now realized he had come to identify as hers, rose to his nostrils and brought such waves of dizziness and desire that he could only hear dimly and vaguely the turmoil about him. His senses returned when the laughter stopped and two of the circle looked up at him curiously. Vicki then threw her head back and looked at him upside down. When her eyes met his, she dropped the glass she was holding onto the rug.

"My God, Morrison, you scared the wits out of me! I thought it was Satan himself. Sit down and join us. Oh, Ann," she said to the tall girl who had followed him from the door, "stop looking at him so hungrily. He wouldn't spit on the best part of you. I've absolutely begged him to make love to me and he won't."

"Vicki, can't we get out of here?" he asked evenly.

"Out?" She swirled around to stare at him. "Where?"

"We have a long-standing date," he answered. "I'll wait outside in the car for you."

Then, to the intense fascination of the group watching the two of them, he nodded politely and vaguely at them, then turned on his heel and went out the way he came in.

In the clubhouse office only fifty feet away from the group, meanwhile, Nelly stared at the figure on the couch.

"Lance, what happened!"

"Is that you, Nelly?"

She kneeled behind the couch where he lay stretched out, his face covered with bandages and handkerchiefs.

"I told them not to call anybody except you," he said, almost with pride. "Only you. They wanted to call my sister in here, but I told them not to even tell her about it. Only you. Nelly, hold me...."

"Oh, Lance, please don't do this to me. Every time I see you.... How did this happen? Why did he beat you up?"

"He did me a favor, Nelly. There's nothing like a good beating that you've been waiting for all your life. Now I don't have to wait for it—I've had it. Nelly, I want you."

"And I love you, Lance. But it hasn't worked for us. You're only coming to me now because you need someone to comfort you. They told me your mother's not here, so you asked for me."

"No, I didn't ask for my mother first. It's not like that."

"You just want to use me for a while."

He shook his bandaged head. "You're so wrong."

"Maybe I'm like a mother to you."

"That's not fair."

She was strangely silent, then she finally breathed, "I'm a stupid person. Here you call for me—after all these years. And what do I do? I try to talk you out of it." She went to him and touched his forehead. "You'd better not be lying to me or fooling me."

"Nelly, I want you, *you*. Life is just disgusting the way it is. Can I leave with you tomorrow morning?"

Her eyes were wet. "Do you mean it, Lance?"

"I mean it."

"Oh, God, I'm so lucky."

He pushed aside the bandage to look at her in wonder, shaking his head. "Not many people would agree with you."

"Something wrong?" he asked as Vicki got into the car. "You look sick."

"No," she said in a soft voice. Did it show that she loved him, that she was afraid of offending him as she always seemed to do?

"Well, you looked white, that's all," he said, starting the car. "I guess it's the drinking you do."

"That's a criticism, I suppose," she said flatly.

He drove silently. She opened her golden purse and brought out a small mirror to peer at her face.

"Why don't you look in the overhead mirror?" he asked.

Yes, she asked herself, *why don't I? I've been sitting crouched at the opposite end of the seat, afraid to move even an inch toward him.*

"Why are you sitting a mile away?" he asked. "Usually you're all over me with your elbows. You're a funny girl tonight."

She looked at her hands. "Nothing's funny. Not anymore."

"No? You were having fun when I barged in on you tonight."

"Well, it only *looked* like fun."

"But still you were ready to leave with me." He seemed to be asking a question. "Why did you leave?"

"Forget it," she said. "Maybe I just like your muscles. Now you can take me to the factory and show me what big muscles you have."

She meant it as an offense, a sarcasm, but he drove steadily and relaxed, and soon they were in front of the factory gate. Mr. Fulton, the watchman, waved at them and opened the gates, then walked away to his shed.

"We've got him trained," Morrison muttered, continuing to drive down to the factory building.

"You trying to drive right inside this place?" she asked as he parked just by the side entrance.

"Doorstop service today." He snapped on the dashboard radio and found a band playing dance music. "And music," he said, with a strange voice.

She glanced up at him for a moment, then got out of the car. He followed and took her arm. They walked into the factory and stood inside. Only a little light came from the parking lights and a red EXIT bulb above the door.

"Aren't you going to turn on the light?" Vicki asked.

"No work tonight," he said. "Just play."

"I see." Her voice dropped. "All right."

She began to open the buttons of her dress. He stepped forward in the darkness, the soft music behind him.

"Where?" she asked, a catch in her voice. "I'm sure you don't have the floor in mind."

"Button that dress, Vicki."

"I don't like hallway stuff," she said stiffly. "I like to be undressed when I play.

"Button it up."

She did so and waited.

"I just want to dance with you," he said.

"Just dance?"

"We have music."

"Yes, we do. All right, dance."

"But we haven't been introduced," he said.

"No...." She smiled sadly. "I think it's kind of late for that."

"Never too late. Here—here's your mother." He stepped to the side. "Now she's introducing us. 'Vicki, this is Mr. Morrison of the Boston Morrisons.'"

"How do you do?" she asked.

"Won't you dance with me, Miss Harper?" He came toward her and took her in his arms. She leaned her body lightly against him. He didn't move. Then they held each other. His lips were fierce and searching as she had always known they would be. He did not stop kissing her and she did not want him to stop. It was she who pulled away finally, drawing herself back from the long pit of oblivion into which his kiss had spiraled her.

"You know something—I love you, you crazy girl," he said. Now his hands were at her dress.

"In the car, in the car," she pleaded. "There's no place here."

They went out to the car and in the faint light from the dashboard and the light reflected by the parking lights, they undressed in the back seat and made love again and again, his cries of satisfaction mingling with hers. Later, she said, "What about Carlotta?"

He shrugged his massive naked shoulders. "She doesn't mean a thing to me. And I'd never mean a thing to her."

"What are we going to do about my mother?"

"She won't be a problem. I think we'll be able to keep her tame from now on."

"No running away? We won't have to?"

"We'll only leave when we want to. When you've got your health, nothing else matters."

She giggled. "That's a funny thing to say."

"I'm full of funny things. I may even ask you to marry me and come to live with me in my world."

"So you've got a world somewhere. I was hoping so."

"Vicki, Vicki...I want you again."

"I can see that," she said, touching his maleness.

Mr. Fulton watched with fascination as their naked shoulders heaved and he heard with delight her wails and the man's groans. He looked on, twenty feet away in the dark, and enjoyed himself thoroughly. He'd never managed to catch them at it before, but of course he'd always known what they were up to.

Published posthumously, *There's No Such Thing as an Inadequate Man* is the second book by Brooklyn, NY-born **Irving Schiffer**. The author was a private investigator who was about to turn the industry on its ear right before he died, a magazine writer and editor, an oil painter, a cartoonist, and a songwriter. Find out more about him in his biography, *Knowing Irv: The Life and Art of Irving Schiffer*. His first book, *A Great Place to Visit: A Political Novel of the 70s* (Arlington House, 1972), is available on Amazon.